JOURNEY FROM THE GREAT PALACE

Robert Wilkinson

TB

Journey from the Great Palace
© 2016 by Robert Wilkinson
Illustrated by David Miles

Published by Deep River Books
Sisters, Oregon
www.deepriverbooks.com

All rights reserved. No part of this publication may be reproduced or transmitted in any form or by any means, electronic or mechanical, including photocopying and recording, or by any information storage and retrieval system, without permission in writing from the publisher. The only exception is brief quotations in printed reviews.

This book is a work of fiction. Names, characters, and events are products of the author's imagination or are used fictitiously. Any resemblance to actual persons, living or dead, is coincidental.

ISBN-13: 9781940269771

Library of Congress: 2015960152

Printed in the USA

Cover design by Jason Enterline

TABLE OF CONTENTS

Introduction.. v

Part 1. The Journey from the Great Palace Begins 1

1. Rachael and the Surprise at the Great Palace................. 3
2. Nighttime and Shepherds...................................... 7
3. The Great Escape.. 13
4. The Journey to Egypt.. 19
5. Rachael and Gabriel Remember the Beginning.................. 25
6. Rachael and Gabriel Remember Adam and Eve................... 29
7. Remembering Passover.. 33
8. Danger in Egypt... 39
9. Returning to Nazareth....................................... 45
10. The Journey to the Temple.................................. 49

Part 2. The Journey from the Great Palace Continues 55

11. Rabbi Eli Goes Home.. 57
12. Jesus Begins His Ministry.................................. 63
13. The Desert... 67
14. Galilee.. 71
15. Samuel and Rebecca... 75
16. The Galilean Ministry Begins............................... 81

17. The Night that Changed Everything 85

18. The Search 89

19. The Touch 95

20. The Tour. 101

Part 3. The Journey Home to the Great Palace Begins 107

21. The Sychar Connection 109

22. The Galilee Controversy. 117

23. Bethesda: A Place of Waiting. 123

24. A Time for Learning. 129

25. Questions, Answers, and Storms. 135

26. Life after John. 141

27. The Lessons of the Storms 147

28. The Rescue. 151

29. Blindness and Sight. 157

30. Life and Death 165

31. The Last Supper. 171

32. Gethsemane 177

33. The Long Night 181

34. Golgotha. 189

35. Saturday. 197

36. Sunday. 201

37. Bible Passages for Further Study. 209

38. About the Author. 217

Introduction and Suggestions for Deeper Study

Angels are amazing beings. God created them, and there are tens of thousands of them. They are incredibly intelligent, yet they don't know everything. They have many jobs to perform, and they possess amazing strength. Though they are usually invisible to man, they can, at times and for special purposes, take on the form of humans.

Scripture only tells us the proper names of four angels. Two are good and two are bad. *Gabriel*, whose name means "God's mighty one," and *Michael*, whose name means "Who is like God," represent the good.

Of the two not-so-good angels, one has two names, *Abaddon*, in Hebrew, or *Apollyon*, in Greek, both mean "destroyer." Probably the best known, however, is *Lucifer*, meaning "shining one," who later became Satan.

Though angels have no gender and their names imply masculinity, femininity should not be discounted completely simply because the Bible is silent on the matter. Indeed, some of their tasks, when placed in the cultural context of Bible times, such as the care of children, line up more on the feminine side. As a result, we do not see that having an angel named Rachael would present a scriptural difficulty.

In this story series, every attempt is made to be faithful to Scripture, history, science, geography, and known facts. When dealing with Scripture, a natural, literal interpretation is chosen. This is a work of fiction woven into actual history. For example, at times words are attributed to Jesus that He may never have said. Close analysis, however, should reveal that in each case they are words that are consistent with His character and personality.

This is a story designed for young readers. It's a tale of an angel named Rachael who becomes involved in the incarnation and life of Jesus. It's a love story—a narrative that gradually develops the gospel and a tale that brings to life two worlds humans are unable to experience—Heaven and the world of Jesus' time. We pray that this story will delight those who read it, both young and old, drawing them into a deeper love and respect, not only for the Scriptures but also for the God who authored them and came to give Himself for us.

Though this story is a work of fiction, it is based on the true stories found in the Bible.

In order to get the most out of this book, the reader may find it helpful to read *Journey from the Great Palace* first. Once this is done, go back and read the actual stories themselves in the Bible. At the end of the book are Bible references that will assist you as you do this. Now, as you read these stories in the Bible, they should seem familiar and alive as you remember them from *Journey*, and recall the lessons they teach. As you read, we urge you to ask questions and "search the Scriptures to see whether these things be so."

It is our prayer and hope that *Journey from the Great Palace* will bring you closer than ever to our Lord and Savior Jesus Christ who actually did make this journey for you.

PART 1

The Journey from the Great Palace Begins

1

Rachael and the Surprise at the Great Palace

"What's all the commotion about?" asked Rachael, one of the smallest angels in Heaven.

"Why don't you ask Gabriel?" another angel suggested. "He's right over there, and he knows just about everything."

So Rachael flew across the golden street to ask Gabriel exactly what was going on. "What's all the excitement about Gabriel?" she asked. "Is someone having a party?"

"God Himself has invited all the angels to a special meeting at the Great Palace," Gabriel answered.

Rachael's eyes grew wide. "The Great Palace! May I come?"

"You're an angel aren't you?" Gabriel smiled.

"Well, yes, I am," she said, "but I'm not really important like you."

Gabriel was one of the two most important and powerful angels in Heaven, even though there were thousands and thousands of them.

"Everyone is important, Rachael," Gabriel said, looking at her. "You are very important to God. Look, why don't you come with me?"

Rachael could hardly believe her ears. Not only was she going to the Great Palace, but she was going with Gabriel. She would never ever forget this day.

On the way to the Great Palace, she asked Gabriel what was so important that all the angels were being invited.

"God will be there, and He will tell you all about it," Gabriel replied. "Just be patient."

Rachael tried to be patient, but patience was something she was not very good at.

"Will Jesus be there?" she finally asked.

"Of course," Gabriel replied. "The Father, Jesus, and the Holy Spirit will all be there."

When Rachael and Gabriel arrived at the Great Palace, most of the angels were already there and God the Father was about to speak. "I would like to share with all of you something that will soon happen," He said. Then, looking across toward His Son He said, "Jesus will be leaving us for a while."

The angels stood in stunned silence. Then they began to murmur. Finally, an angel asked, "Leaving us? Where is he going?"

"To earth," God said. "He is going to become a man."

Every angel in Heaven gasped. "A man. How unthinkable! Is this possible? You have seen what they are like . . . the things they do. They are mean and thankless and say the most awful things. Jesus can't go. He can't."

Then, Jesus stepped up to speak, and Rachael leaned forward as far as she could to hear what He would say. Great tears welled up in her eyes. She could not understand why Jesus would go to earth and leave Heaven . . . and her. Even though Gabriel was nearby, she felt lonely already. Jesus had never gone away before. It was just too much, and she began to sob uncontrollably.

Gabriel saw her and, placing his hand on her shoulder just above her wings, whispered, "Shhh now. It will be OK. He'll be back before you know it."

Just then, Jesus looked straight at Rachael and Gabriel and said, "I know you will miss Me and I will miss you too, very much! But I must go because it is the only way I can show humans how much We love them. One of the reasons people on earth behave as they do is that they don't know Me. I will become a baby. Gabriel has already spoken to Mary. She is a good girl who is living in Nazareth now and We have chosen her to be my earthly mother. She and Joseph will be married soon and be good human parents for Me."

"Mary and Joseph!" Rachael cried out, "I know them. They're poor people. Nobody will ever let them bring you into a palace to look after you there."

"You're right, Rachael," Jesus said. "They are poor, but I will not be born in a palace. In fact, I will never even live in one while I am on earth. If humans are going to understand My love for them, I cannot go to them as a King."

"But they will not understand."

"Some will and some will not," Jesus replied. "I will show My love to all people. Some will receive it and some will not."

Rachael was almost frantic now. Not caring what the other angels thought, she blurted out her worst fears. "Oh Jesus, You know what they are like. They have killed good people, even your prophets. What will they do to you if you don't go as a King?"

"They will kill Me too," Jesus said softly, and Rachael became almost dizzy as she tried to take in what she was hearing.

"Why?" she tried to ask, but her voice was only a whisper. "Why must they do this to you?"

"Come here, little one," Jesus said, and He scooped her up in His arms. "The time will come soon when

Jesus comforts Rachael.

I will pick up human children like this," He said with a smile. "And when I do, I will think of you. Will you keep a secret until I return?" He asked. Rachael nodded her head. "You know, Rachael, that from the beginning of time, humans have broken My laws and not done the things I have asked. Even though I have punished them at times, they can never really pay for the things they have done. The reason I must go to earth is that I must pay the price for humans' sin. Satan hates Me so much he will have Me killed. When that happens, I will pay the price for their sin Myself. Once that price is paid, anyone who trusts Me and asks, will be set free from the guilt of all they have done. I will become their Savior, just as the prophets have already written in the Scriptures. The time will come, Rachael, when millions of humans from all over the world will join us here in Heaven because of what will happen on earth. Can you understand? I will be their gift of life from God!"

While tears still slid down Rachael's face, a little smile also broke through. Jesus knew she understood enough.

As He put her down, He turned to her again and asked, "Rachael, when I am born, there will be some shepherds in a field who will need to know where to find Me. Will you promise to help them find Me?"

2

Nighttime and Shepherds

It seemed that the meeting at the Great Palace had just finished when everyone saw God the Father, the Holy Spirit, and Jesus leaving through the gates of the Holy City.

Rachael and her friends watched them go, knowing that something very important was happening but not knowing exactly what. For the first time ever, soon Jesus would no longer be in Heaven with them, and it felt lonely already.

As Rachael watched, a cloud slowly formed and surrounded both Jesus and the Holy Spirit. She watched and watched but soon could see nothing through the thick cloud swirling about them. There was not a sound as she hovered quietly in place, watching and searching to see anything she could.

What was happening? she wondered. *What's going on?*

And then suddenly it was over. The cloud was gone and so was Jesus.

A feeling of panic began to spread over her as she stared at the empty place where Jesus had just been.

What had just happened?

Suddenly Rachael felt a hand on her shoulder and heard a soft voice in her ear.

"Gabriel!" She exclaimed. "Where did you come from?"

Gabriel didn't answer her question. "Mary is now Jesus' mother," was all he said.

Rachael understood. It had happened. Promises made hundreds of years ago had just been fulfilled, and she had watched it.

Jesus was now a baby. A human baby. Amazing.

As time passed in Heaven, in the land where the angels lived, Rachael found herself busy with things that needed to be done. Human children needed to be watched and protected; a job Rachael loved doing almost more than anything. The times she spent at the Great Palace, praising God and remembering the amazing things He had done, were always wonderful, but without Jesus there, things just seemed to be different. Almost six months of earth time had gone by since Jesus had left, when Gabriel again found Rachael.

Breaking into her thoughts he asked, "Would you like to come with me to tell Jesus' earthly father Joseph not to worry?"

Rachael was shocked at the honor of being asked to attend such an event.

"When?" she asked.

"Now," he replied.

Joseph, a young carpenter, had been worried sick about Mary since he had found out she was going to have a baby. He knew that he was not the baby's real father and didn't know what to do about it. *What had really happened?* he wondered.

Mary had told him that an angel had visited her. The angel had said that God was the real father, but that seemed so ... impossible. He was even losing sleep about it now.

What should he do?

He had finally fallen asleep among the wood chips in his workshop when Gabriel and Rachael arrived by his bed. Without waking him up, Gabriel spoke to him in a dream.

"Joseph," Gabriel spoke softly.

Joseph stirred. Even though he was still asleep, he could see Gabriel standing there speaking to him. Something told him this was no ordinary dream but real. *What's happening?* he wondered.

"Joseph," Gabriel said again. "Don't be afraid to marry Mary as you have planned. The baby she will soon deliver is indeed from God. When He is born you will call His name Jesus because He will save His people from their sins."

Nighttime and Shepherds 9

Gabriel and Rachael tell Joseph about Mary.

Rachael could see Joseph begin to relax as he heard Gabriel's words, and slowly a quiet smile began to cross his face. Now he knew for sure that Mary had been telling the truth. He and Mary could now be married and he would be the earthly father of a Boy named Jesus.

Now that Joseph had been told about Mary and the baby, Rachael remembered her promise to Jesus before He had left the Great Palace. When Jesus was born, she was supposed to tell the shepherds about it and where they needed to go to find Him. The only problem was that she didn't know where that was going to be. She wanted to announce His birth in a royal way because He was a king, however He had told her He wouldn't be born as a king. So she went to Gabriel again for help.

"Gabriel," she asked, "where will Jesus be born?"

"It is already written in the Scriptures," Gabriel replied. "Bethlehem is where the prophets said it will happen."

"But Mary and Joseph live in Nazareth," Rachael said. "How is God going to work that out?"

"Already done," Gabriel said. "Caesar Augustus, even now, is planning a way to tax his people, and he needs to count them. This will make Joseph and Mary leave home and go to Bethlehem, the city where Joseph's family is from. I'll be looking out for them on the way. You will tell the shepherds on the hills near Bethlehem."

Rachael was excited now. This was her opportunity to be a part of something really important, and she wanted to do her best. She could hardly wait.

Finally the day arrived.

Gabriel and some of the other angels had been carefully watching and protecting Joseph and Mary on their long trip to Bethlehem. It had taken more than three days, and several times the angels had protected them from robbers who would have hurt them if they could.

Meanwhile, Rachael had practiced what she would say to the shepherds over and over again, until her friends were beginning to get tired of hearing it. But now the time had finally come.

Only moments ago, Jesus had been born in a dirty stable with cows and sheep all around Him because there was no room for His family to stay in any of the crowded inns.

Rachael still felt that this was no way for the King of kings to be born, but as soon as she saw Him, she forgot all about that. He was such a beautiful baby.

Now she had work to do. She had already located the shepherds in a nearby field and her friends were waiting for her to get back to them so they could begin.

Rachael returned to her friends and, without hesitation, gave the signal to start.

As she raised her arm, suddenly a blazing, warm light flooded the cold, black night. It was as if a curtain of darkness had been rolled away. Behind it, the sky had been turned into fire.

The shepherds became terrified at the sudden explosion of light onto the field that had been so quiet and dark; all except the one young boy who was with them that night. He didn't seem to be afraid at all as he looked up into Heaven and saw Rachael and her friends there. He had never seen her before, yet he seemed relaxed at the sight of her. In a strange way it was as if they knew each other. She recognized him immediately as one of the children she had guarded and kept safe from time to time.

Even though Rachael was small for an angel, she appeared to the shepherds as a huge Angel of the Lord. The very sight of her caused them to cower in fear.

Speaking to the shepherds she said, "Do not be afraid, for I bring you good news of great joy for all people. For unto you is born this day in the City of David a Savior who is Christ the Lord. And you shall find the baby wrapped in swaddling clothes and lying in a manger."

As soon as Rachael had said this, her friends began praising God with loud, beautiful voices, just as they had done at the Great Palace in God's presence. The whole night became as bright as the sun. All around the field the air was flooded with the most beautiful sound anyone had ever heard.

Just as the shepherds were beginning to relax and enjoy the angels and the most amazing events of their lives, Rachael moved her arm and the cold night fell over the shepherds again like a huge wave on the ocean.

Suddenly the light was gone. The angels were gone. The bleating of the sheep was the only thing that broke the silence of the night. But Rachael wasn't gone. Behind the night sky she watched as the shepherds tried to understand what had happened.

She continued to listen to their excited conversation and then smiled as they rose to their feet, turned, and made their way to the stable to see the baby Jesus.

She watched as the young boy still searched for her in the sky, hoping to see her one more time.

For thousands of years people would remember this night and wonder what it was like, and she had been part of it.

This really was a night she would never forget.

3

The Great Escape

Many months had now passed since that amazing night in Bethlehem when Jesus was born. Though Rachael kept busy with things that needed to be done, her mind kept going back to the things that had happened that night in Bethlehem.

Joseph and Mary had now taken Jesus back to Nazareth. There, family and friends fussed over the new baby and life seemed to be getting back to normal. Unfortunately, that would not last long.

Rachael spent her time watching over her children and protecting them, especially the young shepherd boy. He had such a kind heart. He loved to tell his story about the night when baby Jesus was born. Rachael liked him.

Many miles away, kings from Persia were traveling toward Jerusalem. These men were not ordinary kings but priestly kings called "Magi." They knew what the Bible said and understood its promises that one day the Messiah would come and that He would be known as the "King of the Jews."

Finally the Magi arrived at Jerusalem. Upon entering the gates of the city, they were sent to King Herod who wanted to know why they had come.

They responded with a question of their own. "Where is the child who has been born King of the Jews?" they asked.

Hearing this, Herod became furious.

Wasn't he, Herod, King of the Jews? Who was this "King" these Persian dogs were looking for? Why would they insult him by suggesting there was another king besides him?

"We have seen His star in the east and have come to worship Him," they explained.

Worship Him? They need to worship me, Herod thought.

He wanted to throw these men out of his palace and have them killed right now. It would serve them right. But then a thought came to him. Why not use them to find this "King," and then he could fix this problem once and for all?

"So when did you first see this star?" he asked as kindly as he could; although for Herod, being kind wasn't something that he found easy to do.

"Just about two years ago," they replied.

Good, thought Herod. *Now I know how old the child is.*

"Why don't you go and look for the child," Herod suggested, "then, when you find Him, let me know so I may worship Him too." The very thought of worshiping anybody almost made him sick, but he had to appear nice. *Ugh.*

So the Magi left and continued their search, traveling toward Bethlehem. Meanwhile, Herod began plotting how he would kill the child.

"As soon as these 'wise men' tell me where to find him, we'll see who the real 'King of the Jews' is." Herod laughed. He thought this would be so easy. Maybe he should kill the child's parents too. Yes, that would be perfect.

But Herod did not know that Rachael, who had been watching over one of the children who lived in the palace, had heard the whole plan.

Soon after the Magi had left Herod's palace, they spotted the star again and followed it as it moved toward Bethlehem. This was where the prophet Micah had said the child would be born, so it made sense to go there. But when they reached Bethlehem, they noticed that the star kept on moving. Gradually, it turned north, leading them all the way to Nazareth; then, as they reached the city, it led them straight to the place where Jesus was.

Joseph and Mary were astonished to see these wealthy and important kings arrive at the door of their poor home. Getting down from their camels, the Magi fell down on their faces, worshiping Jesus and giving Him their expensive gifts of gold, frankincense, and myrrh.

Rachael was stunned when she heard about Herod's plan to kill Jesus. She knew Herod was cruel, but to kill a baby was unthinkable.

Jesus had told her before He left Heaven that He would be killed, but she didn't think it would be so soon. She had to tell someone and knew just who it would be. So off she flew as fast as she could.

Gabriel was not far from the Great Palace.

"Gabriel, Gabriel!" she cried out. "King Herod plans to kill Jesus. We have to stop him."

"God already knows about this Rachael," Gabriel said. "He has a plan and wants your help."

"Of course I'll help," Rachael replied breathlessly. "But we have to move quickly. Herod could find Jesus at any time."

Gabriel then told Rachael what God wanted her to do.

As Joseph and Mary sat and listened, the Magi told them about their journey to see Jesus. One night as they watched stars, suddenly, a great burst of light appeared in a group of stars called Virgo, meaning "the virgin." When the star started to move, they knew they had to follow it, and so they did.

Mary was amazed! God really was in control; He even controlled the stars.

After their visit to see Jesus, the Magi left and began their trip back to Jerusalem. Little did they know about Herod's evil plan to kill the child.

As the Magi reached the place where they would camp for the night, Rachael was waiting. Finally, after they had talked about all the things that had happened to them on their journey, they went to sleep so they would be rested for the morning.

Rachael moved in close to them and quietly spoke into their dreams.

"You must not go back to see Herod," she said. "He is an evil man and only wants to kill Jesus. You must go straight home instead of going to Jerusalem."

The men awoke from their dreams with a start. All of them had heard the same message. They all agreed. They must stay far away from Herod.

When morning came, the Magi arose, mounted their camels, and headed for home, careful to stay as far from Herod as possible.

It did not take Herod long to learn that the wise men had fooled him. He became so angry that it was not safe to be around him. He screamed and yelled at everyone. He threw things.

"I'll kill them all!" he screamed. "No one will be king but me!" Turning to his men he commanded them, "I want that child dead!"

He threw a candlestick at one of his servants who jumped out of the way just as it crashed into a tray of food.

"Get out now, all of you, and don't come back until you have that child!"

Rachael had to perform one more task to complete the plan that Gabriel and God had in place. And so it was that she arrived at Joseph and Mary's house.

Jesus was asleep. Rachael looked at Him. How different He looked as a small child. She remembered Him as the mighty King in Heaven. It was strange to see Him like this.

When He was in Heaven, He protected and loved her. Now she protected and loved Him. A tear formed in her eye. But, again, she had work to do.

Joseph slept as Rachael approached his bed. She spoke carefully to him so he would remember everything.

"Joseph," she said, "get up now. Take Mary and Jesus and go to Egypt where Herod can't find you. Even now he is trying to find your child to kill Him."

Joseph awoke almost immediately. He had had this kind of dream before, and he knew he must act quickly. He woke Mary and told her the things Rachael had said. Together they gathered Jesus and as many of their things as they could carry and left for Egypt.

The trip would be long, but they would be safe there. The gifts of gold and spices the kings had given to them would be used to pay for the expensive journey. God had given them a special child. God had warned them of danger. God had provided the money for their escape. Rachael watched as they left. They would not be alone. She would be with them, and she would watch over them very carefully.

4

The Journey to Egypt

When the wise men had visited Joseph and Mary, they had given them expensive gifts of gold and spices. But in such a small town, once people knew what had happened it did not take long for a man called Belial to hear about the gifts.

Belial was a thief and a robber who only cared about himself. He had always wanted to be rich and now it seemed to him that God was giving him the chance he had always dreamed of.

Belial knew the man's name was Joseph and that he was a poor carpenter who had just been given some gold by faraway kings. He also knew where Joseph lived. That night he would break into Joseph's home and steal whatever he could. If he had to hurt someone, who would care? Surely no one would be upset at the loss of a poor carpenter or his wife.

That night, he crept to a back window of Joseph's house. With a knife in his hand, he eased his way into the small room. Carefully, he looked around, but there was no one home. No one at all. The house was empty, and they had taken the money with them. From a darkened corner, Rachael smiled. Belial would have to wait to become rich.

Joseph and Mary were already moving slowly along the coast of Palestine, making their way south toward the sea town of Joppa. Many years ago, a man named Jonah had fled from Joppa on a ship while disobeying God. Now years later, Joseph and Mary fled toward Joppa while obeying God.

For the most part, Joseph led the way as Mary, riding on a small donkey, carried Jesus who was now two years old. Whenever they stopped to rest, He would toddle through the grass to the shore, where He would play in the sand and chase the birds.

Invisible to human eyes, Rachael watched Jesus play. It was fun to see Him running, skipping, falling in the sand, and picking Himself up again. The trip was going well. The little family seemed safe for now, but Rachael had an uneasy feeling that they had not seen the last of Belial or his friends.

Early on the third morning, they could see the town of Joppa in the distance. As soon as they arrived in Joppa, Joseph would pay for their trip to Alexandria in Egypt. Here they would board the ship that would take them far away from evil king Herod.

Meanwhile, Belial was furious that he had missed his chance to steal the gold and riches from Joseph and his family. As he asked the people of the town about the family and where they had gone, someone said he had seen them heading south toward Joppa.

"Of course," thought Belial. "With all that money they're going to go on a trip with that child of theirs." Maybe with some help from his friend Nahash, he could still find this family and get his hands on their treasure.

Within the hour, Belial and Nahash had set off toward Joppa. They could easily get there before this man and his wife, who would be slowed down by their child. All they needed now was a plan.

The Joppa market was full of people. Everyone was talking, laughing, moving, and buying things. Joseph and Mary would need supplies for their trip, so they too moved and bumped along with the crowd in search of things to buy.

"Oranges, figs, dates, olives!" cried the sellers behind the stalls. Joseph thought it was exciting to be in this busy place, though soon they would need to head toward the ship bound for Alexandria.

Now, loaded with food and supplies for the journey, they left the market and headed toward the ship. Just as they turned a corner by an empty stable, two large men suddenly stepped in front of them. They were dirty and sweaty. They were also the strongest, meanest, most dangerous men Joseph had ever seen.

"Well, here you are!" sneered Belial, grinning at them through his stained yellow teeth. "We've been waiting for you."

"What do you want with us?" Joseph asked.

"What do you think we want?' Belial replied. "We want the gold and treasure you have been carrying around for the past three days. Now, get into the stable."

Nahash moved toward the donkey and ripped open a large bag. "Here it is!" he yelled excitedly. "There must be a fortune in here."

"We'll take the donkey and kill the rest of them here in the stable where nobody can see. Then we'll get out of here before someone shows up," Belial ordered.

Both men pulled knives from their belts and moved toward Joseph and Mary. Joseph moved in front of Mary and Jesus to protect them, but even as he did, he knew he would lose the fight. They had knives. He did not. They were fighters. He was only a carpenter. There were two of them, but only one of him. Yet still he had to try.

"Get back!" He said to his wife. Holding Jesus, Mary took a step back from the men. Now Joseph turned and faced the two robbers. It was time to fight. But first his family needed to escape. "Now run, Mary!" He yelled.

"Drop the knives immediately!" said a voice from the doorway. "You will not touch these people."

In the doorway, there was a tall Roman soldier with his sword drawn and ready. Two more soldiers with swords stood behind him. Belial's and Nahash's knives crashed to the floor as they lifted their hands in surrender.

Joseph and Mary turned to see the tall soldier. "I'd say that was close, wouldn't you?" the soldier asked, grinning at them.

"Yes it was. Thank God and thank you," Mary replied, panting for breath as she realized they were now safe. Her knees were so weak she almost fell to the ground. The tall soldier gently held her up until Joseph could take her.

"You have a special child there," the soldier said, smiling at Jesus. "We need you to take care of him for us. You need to go now.

Beliel and Nahash receive a surprise.

The ship for Alexandria is leaving soon. We will take care of these men."

"I can't thank you enough," Joseph said. "By the way, how did you know we needed help?"

"We are trained to know what to watch for," the soldier replied with a smile.

As Joseph and Mary went to the ship, Joseph asked, "How did they know we were taking the ship for Alexandria?"

Mary looked at Joseph and shook her head as if to say "I have no idea." Then she asked, "And what did they mean by telling us to 'take care of Him *for us*?"

Joseph thought but remained silent.

As they boarded the ship, Joseph asked, "Mary, who do you think those soldiers were?"

As Belial and Nahash stood trembling before the soldiers, the tall one spoke to them. "Do you know the penalty for attempted murder and robbery?" he asked sternly.

"Yes," they responded together, their voices shaking.

"Well, maybe you should consider following God and turning from evil before it is too late. Riches in heaven are more valuable than riches on earth," the tall one said. "God, who has shown you great mercy, will be watching you, and so will we."

And then suddenly before their eyes, all three soldiers vanished from their sight. Rachael and her angel friends Naomi and Gideon watched as Belial and Nahash collapsed to the floor shaking in terror.

A few moments before, it had been Rachael who appeared as the tall soldier while Naomi and Gideon appeared as the other men who were with him. Rachael smiled. Sometimes appearing as humans could be really cool, she thought.

The angels had clearly warned Belial and Nahash. Instead of punishing them for what they had done they had now been given a fresh chance to change their ways, to do what is right and follow God.

Joseph, Mary, and Jesus were now safely on the ship heading for Egypt.

Soon Rachael would have another errand.

5

Rachael and Gabriel Remember the Beginning

Rachael, Naomi, and Gideon hovered on their wings and watched as the ship carrying Joseph, Mary, and Jesus sailed slowly away from Joppa to Alexandria, Egypt.

They had never been on a ship before. Jesus loved it when the other passengers fussed over Him and played with Him. Rachael had closely watched over them, but now she needed to leave Naomi and Gideon in charge of that and get back to the land of the angels.

Upon her return, Rachael spoke with Gabriel. It was good to see him again. "I watched the boat leave Joppa," Rachael said. "They should be arriving in Egypt just about now."

"Good," Gabriel replied. "It won't be long before Herod dies. When that happens, it will be safe enough to be able to tell them to come back home."

"What will happen to Jesus?" Rachael asked. "He told me He would have to die, but I just don't know how or when. All I know is that it has something to do with being a sacrifice that will allow people to come into Heaven."

"That's just it Rachael," Gabriel said. "We're only angels. We don't know the future unless God tells us what it is. It's still a mystery. We know that what's happening is important but we just don't know the details yet."

Because God created the angels many years ago, before He created people, they could remember things that people could only read about in the Scriptures. As Rachael and Gabriel talked, they remembered things that had happened long, long ago. Rachael remembered them as if they had just happened yesterday.

Looking back, she remembered how Lucifer, the most handsome, intelligent, and powerful angel in all of Heaven, began causing trouble among the angels. He had become angry with God and wanted the other angels to listen to him instead. Nothing like this had ever happened in Heaven before and Rachael hadn't liked it one bit.

Only a short time before this, all of the angels had cheered and shouted with joy because of what God had done. He had created the world with its sky and seas. He had created plants and trees and birds and fish. He had created planets and stars and had placed them in a universe that was so huge that Rachael could not even imagine it. He had created animals. Finally he had created people. Rachael had never seen such amazing things. She had cheered and clapped her hands with joy as she had watched all creation come together from nothing.

Even Lucifer had been amazed with God's creation at first, but now he seemed different. He was angry and proud. He was not the most important being around anymore. He had lost all the attention he seemed to need.

As his anger grew, he began to form an evil plan. He would convince the angels to support him. He would demand that God let him rule this new creation.

"Yes," he thought. "I can do anything. I will be like God."

And so it was that Lucifer met with the angels to get their support for his wicked plan. He promised that as soon as he was in control, he would give them power and glory and fame in this new world. He promised to give them whatever they wanted if they would only follow him.

Some angels agreed with Lucifer and said they would be on his side. Others, like Gabriel and Rachael, said "No way" to his plan. They would stay with God no matter what Lucifer promised.

Now, with thousands and thousands of angels on his side, Lucifer decided it was time to meet with God and give Him his list of demands.

"I am tired of how You are running things here and in this new world You created," Lucifer began. "I think You have taken on too much. Now I am the only one who can help You."

"Here are my conditions," he spouted at God, who quietly listened to every word.

"I will rule with You in heaven," he began. "I will be worshiped in the Great Palace.

"I will be the one who now makes the rules and decides how things are done. I will rise above the clouds and nothing will be above me. I will be the strongest strong one, equal to You."

Lucifer smiled to himself. God needed him, he thought, and these were his conditions. He would show God how things should be done, and Jesus couldn't do a thing about it.

Then God spoke. "You will not rule over My creation, and I will not share My glory with you. You can never be equal to Me. Soon you will be locked in Hell, and you will never escape. The day will come when you will be placed in the lowest parts of the Pit because of this evil plan of yours."

And with those words, as Rachael and the others watched, Lucifer and every angel who had joined him were banished and sent away from Heaven forever.

As Lucifer and his angels fell from Heaven, streaks of light like thousands of giant meteors came crashing down, filling the night sky. No one had ever seen anything like this happen before, in earth or even in Heaven.

God would never allow them to live in freedom again with the other angels as they had before. They wanted to rule the earth so now they would have their chance. Now, everyone would know them as "fallen angels." Lucifer would never be called by his name again. From now on he would be simply known as "Satan."

From a beautiful new garden, the only man and woman in the world stared in excited amazement at the incredible shower of stars before them. Adam and Eve felt no fear as they watched the night sky, for they had no idea that these events would soon rock their world forever.

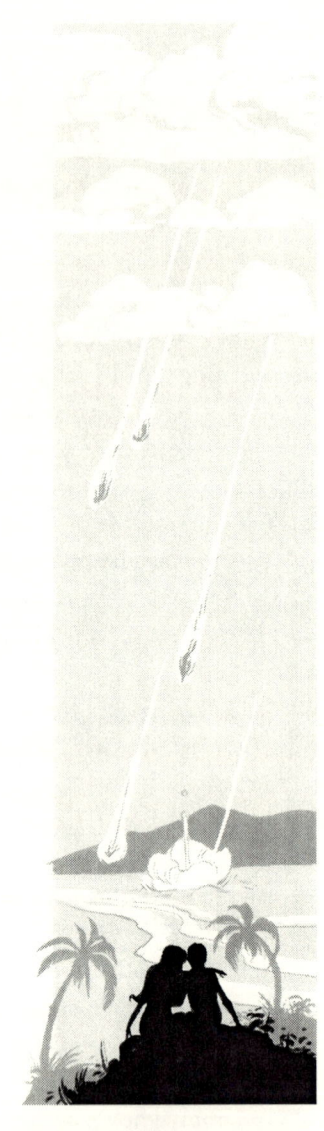

Adam and Eve watch the
star shower.

6

Rachael and Gabriel Remember Adam and Eve

Rachael and Gabriel shuddered as they remembered that awful day when so many angels had followed Satan out of Heaven. She wondered why they had turned against God like that. Sin had touched Heaven, and God had to remove it before it polluted everything.

Satan and his angels were now roaming the earth. They were angry that God had kicked them out of Heaven, and everyone knew it would not be long before they would try to destroy the man and his wife.

God had reached into the dust of the Garden of Eden and with His hand, formed Adam, shaping him into the man He wanted him to be. Then, knowing that Adam would need another human who would understand him and be like him, God then put him to sleep and formed and shaped Eve from his side. When they awoke, God was there, letting them know that they were now husband and wife and that He loved them and wanted them to enjoy their lives with each other and with Him.

Satan couldn't care less about Adam or Eve, but he knew that God loved them and anything God loved, Satan now hated. All Heaven watched to see if the man and woman would be able to stand up to Satan's attack when it came. It did not take long.

God had given Adam and Eve a garden as their home, and it was beautiful beyond words. Everywhere there were flowers bursting with color and trees bearing all kinds of fruit. Every animal and bird that God had created roamed free and unafraid. Lions, tigers, and even dinosaurs were gentle and careful not to hurt anyone. There was no pain, hurt, fear, or worry. There was no death or tears. There was no hate, anger, or selfishness and even God Himself spent time with Adam and Eve. He was their friend.

In the garden with all its fruit to eat, God had shown Adam a tree, called "the tree of knowledge of good and evil." God told the man that he and his wife must not eat fruit from this tree. They could eat from any other tree, but if Adam or his wife ate this fruit, God said they would die. Adam understood the fruit was poison. He told his wife what God had said so that she too would be careful. Together, the man and woman lived and walked with God without any fear, in the most amazing place in the entire world.

Finally, the day came when Satan saw Eve alone in the garden. With no one near to interfere, he entered the body of a large snake and slithered up to her.

All the angels knew this was a dangerous test but were forbidden to warn Eve or to stop Satan in his evil plan. Rachael remembered holding her breath as she watched, wondering what Eve would do. Satan's plan was simple. If he could only get Adam and Eve to disobey God, then God would have to punish them too, just as He had done to him and the angels that followed him. God had even told Adam that if he disobeyed, he would die. *Fantastic!* So Satan began his plan.

"Has God really said you can eat from all the trees except one?" he asked.

"Yes," Eve replied. "We are not allowed to eat from it or touch it or we will die."

"Nonsense," Satan lied, "you will not die." He continued, "God knows that when you eat it, you will be like Him. You will know good and evil."

Eve looked at the beautiful fruit. It certainly looked harmless enough. Carefully she touched it. Then she slowly ate it. Nothing happened. God must have been fooling her, she thought. Maybe He didn't really mean what He said.

Quickly she called Adam to come and offered him the fruit as well. Explaining how she had eaten some of it and nothing had happened, she urged Adam along, "Go ahead. Try some. It's good." Unbelievably, he reached out, took the fruit, and ate it.

Suddenly, they realized they were not wearing any clothes. Quickly, they grabbed some fig leaves to cover themselves. They were terrified, feeling they needed to hide from God. They had never known fear or guilt before, and it was terrible! What could they do?

Rachael and the other angels who were watching gasped in horror. What had Adam and Eve done? They had disobeyed God. When Lucifer had disobeyed, he had been sent out of Heaven! What would God do now? Why hadn't God allowed them to stop Adam and Eve from this sin? Rachael was now in tears. The man and woman would surely die. If only they had obeyed.

Almost immediately they heard God walking in the garden. As Adam and Eve hid in terror they heard Him call, "Adam and Eve, where are you?"

"Hiding," Adam replied. "I heard you and hid because I was naked."

"Who told you that you were naked?" God asked. "Did you eat fruit from the tree I told you was off limits?"

"Eve gave it to me," Adam pleaded.

"What have you done?" God asked Eve.

"The serpent fooled me," Eve replied.

God had finally heard enough. Just as He had done in Heaven, He had to punish both Adam and Eve for the disobedience that was called sin. Satan had already been cast away and sentenced to death, so God spoke to the serpent first. "You will always crawl on your belly in the dust," He told the snake.

To Eve He said, "You will have children, but it will be painful when you do. Also, you will need to listen to your husband even if you don't want to," He said.

Now God turned to Adam for judgment. "Because you have done this, everything you try to do will be hard and difficult. Then eventually, you will die as I told you."

Rachael watched the man and woman as God judged them for their disobedience. She saw tears stream down their faces. She too was in tears as she watched what happened. In a moment of carelessness, everything was spoiled. They would no longer be able to walk with God as they once had. One day the man, woman, all their children, and even their animals would die because of what had happened.

But as Rachael had heard God judge the woman, she had also heard Him make an amazing promise. One day a Savior would come to make things right again. Rachael did not know how or when this would happen. But God had made a promise, and as surely as His promise of judgment and punishment for their disobedience had come true, He would be true in His promise of hope. One day, He would make things right again.

She watched as the man and woman were forced to leave the garden they loved so much. She watched as other angels guarded the garden with flaming swords to keep the man and woman from ever coming back again.

Sadly, Rachael could only hope the Savior would come soon.

1

Remembering Passover

Rachael and Gabriel continued to talk about things that had happened many years before. As they walked through a garden, not far from the golden street that led to the Great Palace, Rachel remembered the garden in which Adam and Eve had lived. She remembered with sadness how they had been forced to leave because of their sin of disobedience.

"Jesus is the promised Savior, isn't He?" she asked Gabriel.

"Yes, He is." Gabriel replied. "I don't know how God's plan will all happen, but I think it has something to do with the night of Passover."

"I remember that!" Rachael said, lighting up with the memory of it.

"So you remember where it first took place?" Gabriel asked.

"Egypt," she replied immediately.

"Exactly. And where is Jesus now?" he asked again.

"Egypt," she replied. "Do you think that's important?"

"I do," he replied. "Remember what the Passover is all about?"

They both remembered back 1,500 years to that first Passover in Egypt. It was an exciting time.

For 400 years—since the time of the patriarch Jacob—the Jewish people (also called the children of Israel) had lived in Egypt. At first the Egyptians treated them well, but over time they had become slaves to the rulers of Egypt, called pharaohs. The Egyptians forced them to work long, hard hours each day. They had to make bricks the pharaohs used to build their pyramids and palaces. They were beaten, starved, and treated more like things than people.

In their pain, they cried out to God for help, but it seemed as if God was not listening. For hundreds of years, they called and waited and heard nothing. Maybe God had forgotten them. But God had not forgotten them. He had heard every cry from every person and at just the right time, a baby was born. That baby's name was Moses.

Rachael remembered Moses well. The pharaoh who lived at that time had ordered all the Jewish baby boys to be killed, yet she remembered how she had helped save Moses from being drowned in the river. She even made sure he would be rescued by Pharaoh's own daughter who would then raise him in the palace as her son.

Rachael also remembered Moses growing up to be a man and how God called him to leave the palace and help set His people free.

From the time Moses left Pharaoh's palace, forty years in the desert would pass before he was ready to help set the Jewish people free. It would take that long for Moses to learn how to trust God enough to be the leader God needed him to be. Learning to trust God is a very difficult thing to do, but finally the time came when Moses was ready.

First, God commanded Moses and his brother Aaron to go to the Jewish leaders. There they listened to what he had to say and accepted Moses as their leader. With excitement in their hearts, they thanked God that He had finally sent a deliverer to free them from Pharaoh's slavery. Now it was time to go and speak to Pharaoh.

"I am the Lord," God said. "Go speak to Pharaoh, king of Egypt and tell him all that I say to you."

So Moses and Aaron went before Pharaoh. There they demanded that he let the people go and set them free from their slavery.

Pharaoh thought, *If I let these people go, who will do all the hard work around here?* He said, "Who is your God that I should obey Him? I will not let these people go."

God was not surprised that Pharaoh would not let Israel go, and He told Moses and Aaron not to be discouraged. God had plans for Pharaoh.

Again, Moses and Aaron went back to Pharaoh, saying, "God says, 'Let my people go.'" But when Pharaoh said no, Moses told

Aaron to stretch out his staff over the river. Immediately, the water became blood, killing all the fish that lived in it. Yet Pharaoh would not let the people go.

So Moses struck the banks of the river with his staff. Frogs began jumping out of the river onto the land until they even filled the homes and the palace. Yet Pharaoh would not let the people go.

Next Moses struck the dust with his staff, turning the dust into lice, biting and infecting everyone. Still, Pharaoh would not let the people go.

Next, God sent swarms of flies into the houses of Pharaoh and his servants. But Pharaoh would not let the people go.

Moses continued to warn Pharaoh. But because Pharaoh hardened his heart, stubbornly refusing to let the people go, God sent a sickness to the Egyptians' cattle in the fields and they died.

During this time, every plague or punishment that God sent only happened in the Egyptians' homes, fields, and rivers, and did not touch the land of Goshen where the Jewish people lived. Even though Pharaoh saw this, he would not let the people go.

As Pharaoh continued to refuse to let the people go, God sent even more plagues. He sent painful sores that appeared on the Egyptians and their animals. Huge hailstones pounded the Egyptians' fields killing their crops and trees. He sent locusts that sprang up and ate everything in sight that the hail had not killed. Still, Pharaoh refused to let the people go.

Now God sent a darkness that covered the land so that not one person in Egypt could see anything for three days. Still Pharaoh refused to let the slaves go. This time, however, Pharaoh had had enough of Moses, Aaron, and their annoying God. With his face red with anger and fury he was finally unable to stand it any longer. This time when he told them that he wouldn't let the people go, he also screamed at them, "Get out! Get out now! I never want to see your faces again. The day I do, you will die."

Moses looked at him and said, "You never will." Then he turned and left.

Now God would send one more plague and it would be the most awesome and terrible one of all. On the night of the fourteenth day of the month God would send a death angel to pass through Egypt, taking the life of the oldest male child in every home. Only those homes following God's instructions would be spared, and these instructions needed to be followed exactly.

Rachael now clearly remembered that night long ago. She had been watching the children of a man named Simeon when he arrived home that night with exciting news. Soon the final plague was about to come and then they would finally be free. After four hundred years they would no longer be slaves. This night the oldest Egyptian male child in every home would die. Yet, even though this plague was designed for the Egyptians, if any Jewish family did not follow God's instructions, the oldest male child in their home would also die. If, however, a family faithfully obeyed God's instructions, the death angel would pass over their homes and not harm them. This is why the Jewish people called it the night of Passover.

Simeon's wife, Mari, gasped, her hand flying to her mouth when she heard the news. They had two children, Hannah, who was four, and their oldest child Joseph, who was five. They had to follow every instruction God gave them and make no mistakes or little Joseph would die that night. Rachael watched carefully as they prepared.

God had told Moses that each family needed a lamb. It was now the tenth day of the month, with four days to go. Rachael watched as Simeon carefully searched the market stalls for the right lamb. The lamb was to be only a year old and could not have any marks or scars on it at all. It had to be perfect.

Unfortunately, it seemed that he couldn't find a perfect lamb anywhere! Every lamb he saw had some mark or scar. He began to panic as he thought of his only son dying because he could not find a perfect lamb. "Please God," he prayed, "help me find the right lamb for us."

Although Simeon had no idea Rachael was there, gently and silently she guided him around a corner to a new stall he had not seen before. And there it was: a small, white lamb. He checked it closely for marks and scars. This was the most perfect lamb he had ever seen. Rachael smiled as he bought the lamb, lifted it on his shoulders and started for home.

At home, Mari and Hannah worked together. The whole house needed to be cleaned. They had to carefully check each room to make sure there was no leaven, or yeast, accidentally left behind.

Rachael kept an eye on this as well, but Mari and Hannah seemed to be doing fine on their own as they removed all the leaven from the house.

As the fourteenth day of the month arrived, Simeon held the lamb as Mari, Joseph, and Hannah said goodbye to it. They had grown to love the small lamb since it had come into their home four days ago. Now they said a prayer of thanks for the perfect lamb that would die in their place. The children cried as Simeon took it away for the last time. Rachael too was sad as she watched, even though she knew it had to be done.

When Simeon returned that evening, he gave the dead lamb to Mari to prepare it for supper. While she was doing this, Simeon had one more important task to perform. Carefully, according to God's instructions, he took a hyssop branch, dipped it in some of the lamb's blood, and spread it above the front door. This would be a sign to the death angel to pass over the house. Now the house was covered by the blood and protected by God. Because they were only protected if they stayed inside that house, they could not go outside until morning.

That night as they ate their first Passover dinner, they wondered if the angel would pass over their house that night. Had they done everything the right way? Would Joseph be alive in the morning?

No one got much sleep that night. Knowing that they were soon going to be free after all those years of slavery was exciting. But they could also not help worrying about Joseph.

As Rachael watched, Joseph slept peacefully. But in the land of Egypt there was no peace. From where she watched, Rachael felt a chill in the air. Being an angel, she could see what was happening as death moved closer and closer. The sky grew darker, the air became cooler, the earth shook ever so slightly, and a low howl, like a faraway wind, began to grow louder.

In the morning, the cries of mothers and fathers and family and friends could be heard as they discovered the terrible result of Pharaoh's decision to disobey God. Not a single home had been left untouched by death. Everywhere, just as God had promised, the oldest son in each Egyptian family had died. Even Pharaoh looked down at his own son's dead body.

When Simeon and Mari woke up that morning, they rushed into Joseph's room. Had the death angel seen the blood and passed over their home? Rachael watched as they burst in.

"Mommy, Daddy!" Joseph called out from his bed as they rushed to his side.

As Pharaoh grieved in his palace late at night he sent a message to Moses and Aaron for them to come. Though they were not invited to speak with him face to face, they knew he was going to finally let them go. Gone was the pride of before. Gone was the arrogance. Gone was the feeling that he could beat God if he wanted.

"Get out of my country," the message said. "Get out now and take your people with you."

8

Danger in Egypt

Rachael and Gabriel continued to talk about what had happened so long ago in Egypt.

"Do you see why Passover is so important now?" Gabriel asked.

"I think so," Rachael replied, though she was a little unsure.

"Tell me Rachael, who set the Jewish people free in Egypt?" Gabriel asked.

"Moses?" Rachael said.

"True," Gabriel said. "He was the human leader who helped set them free, but who else?"

"God, of course," Rachael continued. "He planned everything."

"Good," Gabriel replied. "We know that Jesus is God. We angels understand that God is the Father, the Son, and the Holy Spirit all in one God because we have seen Him. Humans have a hard time understanding this because they do not know Him the way we do.

"So who else freed the Jewish people?" Gabriel asked.

"Who else is there?" Rachael asked. "Moses, God," she paused, and then it came to her. "The lamb!" she exclaimed. "Without the lamb, they could not be free!"

"Here is the reason why I believe Passover is so important," Gabriel said.

"I believe Jesus will actually be a picture of all three. He will be a deliverer just like Moses. He will be human and come out of Egypt. He is God the Son. But I also believe He will be the lamb. We need to wait now and see how, but Rachael, I know He is the Lamb of God."

"And if He is the Lamb," Rachael whispered, remembering what Jesus had told her, "He will have to die."

As they were talking, Naomi and Gideon returned from Egypt. "Joseph and Mary are now in Egypt and have found a home there," they reported. "They have met new friends there at the synagogue. The people there have accepted them as family."

This was great news. Even though Herod had tried as hard as he could to kill Him, it looked as if Jesus would be safe at last. But Satan had more than one way to try to kill the Savior. He just had to think for a minute, and as he did, a plan began to form.

"Yes," he thought, as a small, evil smile began to form across his lips, "why not?"

As Joseph worked in his carpenter's shop, Jesus played among the wood chips in a safe place where He could be watched. Mary had gone to get water with some friends she had met at the synagogue. God had been so good to them, telling them of Herod's evil plan and helping them escape. They had found friends here and the rabbi at the synagogue was very kind to them. Egypt, they decided, was a good place to be.

No one saw the dark snake hiding by the corner of the woodshed. The snake was an Egyptian cobra, one of the most dangerous snakes in the world. The venom from this snake's bite would kill even a large man in minutes.

The cobra looked at the man and the child playing nearby. It didn't like the noise and chatter, so it began to move. It slithered slowly around the shed, went through some bushes and grass, and slid silently under the house.

That night after supper, Joseph and Mary sat and talked. They remembered all the amazing things that had happened in such a short time. They thought of how their lives had changed and laughed as they remembered the look on Belial's face when the soldier had suddenly appeared. They thought of how much they had grown to love each other, and they thought of how much they loved Jesus, now sleeping in his bed. They did not know that just beneath his bedroom floor, the cobra waited.

In Heaven, Gabriel and Rachael had talked about many things as well. Rachael had really enjoyed getting to know Gabriel over these last few years. She loved learning from him since he was so close to God. She loved being part of the things that were happening on the earth. There was still so much that even the angels didn't know, but they all had a feeling that they would be learning much more very soon.

Naomi and Gideon were telling Rachael about the trip to Egypt and how well Jesus was doing there when Gabriel, who had been called to speak with God, suddenly appeared.

"Rachael, God wants you to go to Egypt right away," he said. "Jesus is in danger. God has given you great authority to protect Him. Now go!"

As the morning sun rose over the land of Egypt, Jesus woke up. The night had been peaceful and quiet, and aside from normal night noises, nothing seemed out of place. Joseph and Mary hugged and kissed Jesus as He crawled into bed with them. Soon it was time for breakfast.

After breakfast, Joseph went to the woodshed to begin his workday. Jesus went into His room to play but soon became lonely. While His mom busily cleaned things, He toddled outside to see His dad in the woodshed. But He was not alone.

Under the bedroom floor, the air was cool; but outside, the sun warmed the earth. This is where the cobra decided it would go to find warmth and again it began to move.

No one saw the deadly, dark snake as it slid from under the house and moved toward the shed. It smoothly slithered through the dust and into the grass. Still hidden, it moved behind a small pile of rocks only a few feet from where Jesus played. The rocks were warm now and the snake curled against them to enjoy the heat.

Satan smiled. This was working out just perfectly. All he needed now was for something to startle the cobra so it would strike.

Unaware of the danger that was so close by, Joseph worked hard in his shed struggling with a heavy piece of wood. Wrestling it over to his bench, he dropped it with a loud crash.

Startled by the noise, the cobra suddenly shot its body up three feet into the air, towering there to see what was happening. The sides of its neck spread out like wings, quivering. Its cold reptilian eyes searched for something to strike. Anything near it was in danger. Immediately it spotted Jesus. Deadly venom surged into its giant fangs. Its hissing mouth opened wide, preparing to snap shut on the child.

As Jesus played with his toys among the woodchips just outside the shed, Joseph reached for a hammer to fasten two pieces of wood together. The hammer paused in the air for a moment and then swung down to the wood. With a bang it struck the nail. In a flash, the cobra jumped and struck at Jesus with all the force it had.

The eye of an eagle can see things that no one else can see. It can see things farther away than any human eye. So it was that an eagle, circling high above the small shed, had detected the movement of a snake as it had moved from the house to the rocks. There was no warning. There was no cry. There was no sound at all except a rush of air as a giant shadow flashed by the shed door! Strong talons grabbed the snake and held on tight only moments before its fangs could reach the

The eagle arrives just in time.

child. Lifting the cobra into the air, the eagle flew up and away from the woodshed. In a moment the snake was gone. Jesus was safe again.

Joseph saw the shadow and heard the brief flutter of wings but never saw the eagle or the cobra. He would never know the danger that had come so close to taking his Son. But that did not mean the event had gone unnoticed.

Rachael had seen the whole thing. She tried to catch her breath as she trembled at the thought of what had almost happened. Tears fell down her cheeks. That had been far too close.

God had given her the power to call the eagle. She had guided it to the small woodshed just in time. She still felt as if she had not done her job as well as she should. She had protected many other children but had almost lost the most important one of all. She would never let that happen again.

Satan cursed as the eagle grabbed his snake. He fumed in anger at that miserable little angel who had ruined everything. Who did she think she was, messing with him like that? But it wasn't over yet, was it? Oh no! He vowed someday he would get that child! Someday he would rid the world of this Jesus.

9

Returning to Nazareth

As news of Herod's death drifted through the land of Israel, most people were overjoyed. Still, many wondered how the future would now unfold.

Though the land of the angels rejoiced as well, their celebration centered not as much over Herod's death, as over Jesus coming back home from Egypt. Rachael was selected to bring the news to Joseph.

As Joseph slept, Rachael again spoke to him through a dream. "Joseph, Wake up. It's time to take Jesus and Mary back to Israel. The people who wanted to kill Jesus are now dead."

When Joseph woke up from his dream, he immediately prepared for the long journey home. They had been treated well in Egypt and had met many wonderful people they would never forget. However, it would be good to finally go home and not have to be afraid of Herod anymore.

As they said their final goodbyes, Rachael hovered on her wings like a small, silent helicopter, watching. She remembered how quickly danger could come, especially if Satan was behind it, so she was being extra careful this time.

There were no snakes and no robbers. The ship they would sail home in looked like it was in good condition. Everything seemed to be safe and ready, and Rachael relaxed a little bit. She knew that even if she missed something, God would be there to take care of it. He was really the one in control, and He could do anything.

Finally, the ship gently pulled away from the port in Alexandria with Joseph, Mary, and Jesus on board. The weather was beautiful for the trip. The sea was smooth, and Jesus' parents enjoyed watching him running and playing on the deck. He quickly became friends with the other passengers, including the captain, who even let Him steer the ship for a while. As the ship glided along on its eastbound course across the blue-green sea, they could see the coastline of Egypt just off the right, or starboard, side. Soon the ship turned slightly north. The land of Israel replaced Egypt off the starboard bow. As the ship approached Joppa, Joseph and Mary began to feel their excitement grow as they realized they were finally home again.

What they did not realize was that Scripture had just been fulfilled as a promise God had made years ago now had actually come to pass. Seven hundred years earlier, the prophet Hosea had written, "Out of Egypt I have called My Son."

Joseph and Mary loaded up their little donkey and began the journey home. When they finally reached a small inn, they stopped for the night. Once they were safely inside, Rachael decided to check on an old friend.

His name was Samuel. He was the shepherd boy who had been in the fields the night Jesus was born. He was fourteen years old now and still remembered the amazing things he had seen that night—the angels praising God and the baby in the manger. Rachael liked him because he had a kind heart. He was gentle and loved to do good whenever he could.

Those who knew him liked him, especially a young girl named Rebecca. Together they would talk for hours and make plans for the future. He would make a good living as a shepherd and already had his own sheep. When he was able to support Rebecca, they would be married.

Rachael smiled. It was good to see him again. She was glad he was well. She liked Rebecca too. She was a beautiful girl, not only on the outside but on the inside as well. They both loved and trusted God, and together they would make a fine couple.

Many people traveled the road from Joppa to Jerusalem. The road was less dangerous than the ones from Nazareth and Jericho.

Starting out at the seacoast with its sandy beaches, the road moved across the lush, flat Plain of Sharon. In the distance they could see the Judean hills. As they traveled, the hills grew closer and closer until the road twisted and climbed, higher and higher, following the rugged terrain eastward to the Holy City. Off to the right, a huge valley appeared. Called the Valley of Sorek, this was the same valley Samson had walked through, many years before, on his way to meet Delilah.

With the valley on their right side, Joseph and Mary would follow it all the way to Elizabeth's home. Mary had gone to her cousin Elizabeth when she first discovered she was going to have a baby. Elizabeth and her husband Zecharias still lived there with their young son John, who was only a few months older than Jesus. After being away so long, it would be good to see them again.

Mary wondered how Jesus would get along with John and if maybe they might even become close friends. She and Joseph had talked about living close to Elizabeth and Zecharias so the boys could grow up together.

When they reached the house, Elizabeth squealed with delight at seeing them. Crying with joy, she ran and threw her arms around them and then scooped up Jesus, holding Him for the first time since He had been a small infant.

John was shy at first, but soon he and Jesus were playing together as if they had never been apart. Mary was glad to see it.

As soon as Zacharias arrived, he and Joseph hugged each other like old friends. Then everyone sat and ate and told stories until late into the evening. There was so much catching up to do!

After the long trip, Joseph and Mary were tired and ready to go to bed. Jesus and John had been sleeping soundly for hours. Finally the time came for everyone to say goodnight and soon all was quiet except for the snoring coming from Zacharias' room.

"Joseph, Joseph," Rachael whispered. "I know you would like to live here close to Zacharias and Elizabeth, but it is still too dangerous. Herod is dead, but his son is now in power here. He will harm

Jesus if he finds out you are here. Continue home to Nazareth where everyone will be safe."

Joseph awoke from his dream. He was getting used to this now and knew exactly what he must do. They could visit here for a while, but soon they must leave. He woke Mary and told her what had just happened. Together they praised and thanked God for His wonderful care. How could they not be amazed at all the things that were happening?

A few days later, tears of sadness and joy streamed down their faces as Joseph, Mary, and Jesus left Zacharias, Elizabeth, and little John to continue their journey home. Jesus and John had become friends, even at such a young age, and it seemed sad that they had to say goodbye now. As they watched the family leave, Elizabeth turned and looked at Zacharias. They did not know where or when, but they both felt sure the two boys would meet again.

It had been three days since Joseph, Mary, and Jesus had left Jerusalem. Now they could see the hills of Nazareth coming into view. Nazareth, located just above the Plain of Armageddon, had once been their home, and so it would be again. As they entered town, no one paid any attention to the man, the woman, the small Boy and the little donkey with dirty feet kicking up dust into the air that rose and gently settled back down again. But Rachael watched.

They would live here. They would raise Jesus as best they could here. They would attend synagogue here. Jesus would learn the Scriptures here. He would play and make friends here. This would be home until the day God called Him. Then His work on earth would begin.

10

The Journey to the Temple

It had been nine years since Jesus and His parents had left Egypt and had returned to Nazareth. Jesus was twelve years old now. He was just another kid from a small town—except for a few small details. As in most things, some people noticed these details and some did not.

Most people did not see that Jesus was not only a good kid, but a perfect one. He never got into trouble. He never disobeyed His parents. He was respectful. He was kind to others. He always stuck up for kids who were being bullied. He always did His chores, and oh, yes, He loved to go to the synagogue and learn the Scriptures.

While most people didn't notice all of these things, one kind, wise, old rabbi in Nazareth named Eli did notice. Eli was the kind of person who not only saw things but thought about them. Everything meant something to Eli. Everything was like a puzzle piece that had to fit together into a bigger picture. And that picture was the Scriptures. And Jesus was the puzzle.

For years, Eli had observed children. He had never seen a child like Joseph's son Jesus, and the more he watched Jesus, the more the puzzle grew.

Jesus not only loved learning the Scriptures, it was almost as if He had been there and written them. As He dealt with others, it was as if the Scriptures guided everything He did. He did not return an evil act with another evil act. He always returned an evil act with a good one.

Yes, Eli had seen many children over the years, and he knew Jesus was definitely not an ordinary child. He had never heard Jesus speak one hurtful word. Not one.

Did not Jeremiah say that the heart of man was evil?

Did not Isaiah say that our sins testify against us?

Did not David write in Psalm 14 that there is no one who does good, not one?

So where does Jesus fit into Scripture? he wondered.

Even though he was a respected rabbi, he knew how often he himself failed to be as good a man as he knew he should be. So he watched and wondered and searched the Scriptures for any information he could find about Jesus.

Nissan, the first month of the Jewish calendar, occurs in early spring and with it the most important feast of all: Passover. This year excitement was running through the family. Because Jesus was twelve years old, He would now go with His parents to Jerusalem and take part in the Passover celebrations.

Jesus was working in the back of the carpenter shop with Joseph when Rabbi Eli stopped by.

"Rabbi, it's good to see you," Joseph said, stepping out of the shop to greet his old friend.

"And you, my friend," the old man replied. "I have come to talk with your Son if I may."

"Of course," Joseph replied. "Jesus, you have a visitor."

Jesus came out of the shop and flashed a wide smile at Eli when he noticed him standing there.

"Such a boy! Always a smile for an old man," Eli exclaimed. "So I hear you are going to Jerusalem for Passover. I wish I could go with you to celebrate, but God has trusted me with this synagogue and I need to be here."

"I wish you could come too, Rabbi," Jesus replied. "Then we could spend the time talking and it would make the trip much shorter."

"Ah, you have your father and mother to talk to," Eli replied.

"But you and I talk about the Scriptures," Jesus said. "I enjoy that."

"Listen, my Son," Eli said, placing his hand on Jesus' shoulder. "When you get to Jerusalem you will find men who know the

Scriptures better than anyone in all of Israel, right there at the Temple. Talk to them. They will answer many questions I cannot. Many of them know every word of Scripture by heart. But do not be afraid of them. Ask them your questions my Son. And when you return, you will come to me and share what you have learned, eh?"

"Yes, Rabbi, I will," Jesus promised.

Eli looked at Joseph and shook his head. "Such a boy," he said as he turned, waved his hand, and left.

The trip to Jerusalem, even without Eli, seemed to go by quickly. Even though Joseph and Mary had made the trip to Jerusalem many times now, they still stopped, looking in awe at the magnificent Temple as it came into view. The sun reflected brightly off the Temple's white walls, its gold, its brass, and its silver, each of which was part of the huge structure.

All around them, pilgrims streamed into the city, some coming from many miles away. Many, bringing with them animals they would sacrifice for their sins, were heading to the massive Temple Mount area. Most, including Joseph, traveled with friends and family in groups. They did this both for fellowship with friends as well as for safety from robbers and thieves.

Joseph, Mary, and Jesus were excited about staying with Elizabeth, Zacharias, and John. They wanted to catch up on each others' lives and learn what had been going on since they had last seen each other.

The meeting with Elizabeth, Zacharias and John was as wonderful and exciting as anyone could have hoped. Jesus and John became immediate best friends again as John showed Jesus the area around their home. Yet, even though they were now with their family in Jerusalem, there was a lot to do to get ready for Passover. The most important thing that needed to be done now was to purchase a lamb. This was Joseph and Jesus' job and they went off to the Temple area to do just that. Both clearly remembered why they were buying a lamb as they thought about the events of that first Passover in Egypt. They were buying a lamb so it would die for them, just as though it were responsible for their sins.

Back at Zacharias and Elizabeth's home, they were preparing the house for Passover. They had gotten rid of all leaven from the house as the Passover law required and were getting the Passover meal ready. They had baked the beaten bread without any yeast and when the lamb had finally arrived, it had been killed.

Everything had been carefully prepared, even what they would drink. Finally, Passover evening arrived and the meal was ready to eat.

When everyone finally sat down for the meal, Zacharias spoke about the purpose of the meal to the family. When he finished the familiar words, everyone finally ate, enjoying this wonderful meal together with family. Soon the supper was finished, and the time for remembering came to an end as they sang a hymn together. Jesus' first Passover in Jerusalem was now over.

As the sun rose the next morning, Jesus did what He had been looking forward to from the beginning. Because they had been so busy getting ready for Passover, He had not yet had the time to talk to the priests at the Temple. Now seemed to be the right time. So Jesus left with John and some friends from home, heading off to the Temple to find the priests. When the boys arrived at the Temple, Jesus left John and His friends and went into the court to listen to the discussions going on all around Him. Before long, Jesus joined the conversations.

The Pharisees were especially proud that they had an answer for everything. One turned to Jesus and asked, "So, young man, do you have any questions for us?"

"I do," Jesus replied. He had been thinking about the Messiah, or Deliverer, that God had promised would someday come to make things right again after Adam's sin. "Does the blood of the lambs we have just sacrificed take away our sin or just cover it? If it takes our sin away, why must Messiah come? If it only covers it, how is it possible for a sinner to be fully forgiven?" They looked at each other in silent amazement. *Who is this boy?* they wondered.

Meanwhile, Joseph and Mary had said their goodbyes to Elizabeth and Zacharias. Thinking that Jesus had already started home with His friends, they began their journey back to Nazareth. A day later, they reached the rest of their family and friends on the road. As they began asking where Jesus was, the frightening news became clear. No one knew. Now they had no choice but to return to Jerusalem to try and find their Son.

Most of the pilgrims were gone now, but Jerusalem was still a busy place. Rachael, who had seen everything that had happened to the family from the beginning, quietly guided the anxious parents to the Temple court area. There, for the past three days, Jesus had been discussing Scripture with the Pharisees and teachers.

Mary's relief at finally finding Jesus quickly turned to anger. She asked him, "Why have you done this to us? We have been worried sick about you!"

The response that Jesus gave came in the form of a question that clearly revealed that even at the age of twelve, He knew He was God's Son. "Did you not know I should be about My Father's business?" Jesus asked. But they did not understand what He was saying.

"Who are you?" one of the priests asked Joseph and Mary. "And who is this Boy?"

"I am a carpenter from Nazareth and this is my Son," Joseph replied.

The priests stared at them in amazement. "We have never seen anything like it," they said. "How does He know these things at such a young age?"

Both Joseph and Mary stared at Jesus and then at each other. "Come on, Son," was all Joseph could say. "We need to catch up with the others."

For many days now, an idea had been floating around in Eli's mind giving him no rest. This idea was the only thing that helped him understand what he was seeing. It seemed ridiculous, of course, but it was the only answer that he could think of. The thought made him tremble in awe and fear. So Eli sent a request to an old friend in Jerusalem about a story he had once heard.

While Jesus was in Jerusalem, Eli heard back from his friend. As he read the letter, he knew the answer would change his life forever.

His friend had known a wise man in Jerusalem, a prophet named Simeon who had died years before. Twelve years ago, this man told everyone that a child had been born. He had seen and held this child. God had shown him, and he believed with all his heart that this child was the promised Messiah.

The rest of the story was what shocked Eli and almost took his breath away. According to Simeon, this child, who would now be twelve, was from Nazareth. Eli would check out this story with Joseph himself, but in his heart he already knew the answer. Jesus was from Nazareth. Jesus was indeed the promised Messiah.

Someone knocked on his door and Rabbi Eli opened it.

"Good morning, Rabbi. I've come to tell you about Passover in Jerusalem," Jesus said.

With tears in his eyes, the old rabbi answered, "Come in, my Son. So this is what it's like to stand in the presence of the Messiah."

Rachael hung on her wings with tears of joy in her own eyes. When humans accept Jesus, believing who He is and placing their trust in Him, the Scriptures say that angels rejoice. Rachael certainly knew this was true.

But now she had to go! God had things for her to do and people for her to protect and help. There were Samuel and Rebecca and others who needed guidance and encouragement.

She would still keep an eye on Jesus and Joseph and Mary. Many more adventures lay ahead for Jesus, and Rachael would be right there watching them.

PART 2

The Journey From the Great Palace Continues

II

Rabbi Eli Goes Home

Many years had passed since those early days in Nazareth, and now Rabbi Eli lay in his bed struggling for breath.

He had lived a good life for eighty years. He had comforted others when they needed someone to care. He had defended those who could not defend themselves and had given selflessly to the poor. He had loved his people here in Nazareth. He had taught them to love the Lord their God and to know the Scriptures. Yes, everyone who knew him loved and respected him. And now he was dying.

Where is Shimon? he wondered. He had sent his son to get Jesus, the son of Joseph, to come and see him. Where were they? They should be here by now.

His family was here with him. Leah, his faithful wife of almost sixty years, knelt by his bed and held a cool cloth to his forehead. His daughters, Ruth, Esther, and Naomi, sat close by as well. Their eyes filled with tears because they knew these were his final hours on this earth.

Suddenly the door opened. Shimon and Jesus entered. Shimon rushed to his father's side to see him and hold his hand once more. Jesus, now a man, stood back and waited. He watched this family that had been so kind to Him during His growing-up years. He struggled with the heavy weight of death that now descended like a dark blanket of sorrow upon their lives.

He knew exactly how they felt. He remembered the death of His own earthly father, Joseph, just two years ago and how it had hurt. He remembered the look of despair on his mother's face. He remembered the ache He had felt that such a good and kind dad had been torn away from them so soon. He had wanted to reach over and heal his dad, but He knew that His time had not yet come. He had needed to let him go. It had hurt and it had felt awful.

Mary seemed to understand. His brothers and sisters did not. In their minds, they wondered why He couldn't heal their dad if He was the Messiah. He could not answer them then, but He did share their pain.

From the time of Adam's sin until now, death continued to ruin lives on earth, and there didn't seem to be any way to escape. Wives wept over the death of their husbands and parents. Husbands held dying wives in their arms. Children cried over friends, family, and even animals that they loved.

With every ruined life, Satan tossed his head back and laughed. Deep inside, Jesus told Himself again, "Not for long, Satan; not for long."

Finally, Eli called Jesus over and whispered, "Who would have thought that a poor rabbi from Nazareth would die in the presence of the Messiah? Such an honor I could never have dreamed of, eh?"

Jesus felt tears forming in His eyes. Rabbi Eli had been the first person in Nazareth to realize that Jesus was indeed the promised Messiah. Rabbi Eli was permitted to tell his family, and together they had kept this secret for many years. Only this family and the family of Jesus knew the story. It was a secret that would be kept until Jesus' time had come and His earthly ministry could begin.

"You are thirty years old now," Eli whispered. "Surely your time is near. How I would have loved to have seen it, but God knows best, eh?"

Jesus nodded. "We will meet again soon, my friend, and when we do, there will be no more pain or tears. You have been like a father to Me. I will never forget you."

Eli coughed, and Leah, though she was nearly eighty years old herself, came immediately to his side to help. Jesus watched as Eli gathered his children and grandchildren together and blessed them, reminding them of who they were. He told them that he was proud of them. He encouraged them to remain faithful to God and to do whatever Jesus asked them to do. With his family holding him close, he looked at Leah and smiled. Then, with his last breath, he nodded at Jesus, closed his eyes, and died.

As she watched Eli die, Leah sobbed softly. Her daughters and grandchildren cried with her, their tears flowing down and mixing together on the floor. Shimon was the man of the family now and holding back tears, he struggled to be strong.

Jesus stayed with them to comfort them and to share their pain. He knew what they were going through. He felt the same pain as well. He had lost a good friend. But He also knew what they could not see and what was happening even at this very moment.

Suddenly, Rabbi Eli's eyes snapped open. Where was the pain? Was it gone? Yes, of course it was gone! He took a breath. It wasn't hard for him to breathe now. He felt young and alive again. He was able to move freely, without any effort at all. His mind was now able to think clearly, as if there was nothing he could not understand.

Suddenly he gasped as he tried to comprehend what he was seeing. Two of the most beautiful and awesome angels he could ever imagine stood in front of him. Their faces shone with light and their skin glowed like polished bronze. Their teeth were as white as fresh snow. Their dark eyes shone with beauty and wisdom. Their clothes were radiant and white and on their backs, wings moved gently as they floated in the fresh air.

"Who are you?" Eli asked.

"My name is Rachael," the smaller one answered. "This is my friend Naomi. We are here to bring you to Paradise."

Eli tried to speak, but he didn't know what to say to these beautiful creatures. He looked back over his shoulder into the room of his house from which he had just come. He saw Leah crying over his old

Rabbi Eli enters Paradise.

and lifeless body. He saw his daughters in tears. He saw the pain on Shimon's face and He saw Jesus moving over to comfort them.

Suddenly, Jesus looked up at Eli with a small smile that said "It's OK, old friend; everything's fine. I will be with your family. Go now with My angels."

Eli looked around the house that he had lived in most of his life. He realized that he didn't live there anymore. Excitement began to fill his heart about what he was going to see! The air around him was fresh and clear, and he could hear the most beautiful music. He nodded at Jesus and turned to Rachael and Naomi.

"Let's go," he said. "I'm ready to go home."

The wind blew through Eli's hair and against his face as he flew with Rachael and Naomi toward a land of light. It felt as if only a few seconds had passed before they descended through a cloud. Below them was a beautiful garden that seemed to have no limit to its size. Gently they landed in front of a large gate.

"Where are we?" asked Eli.

"This is your new home," Rachael answered. "There are some people who want to see you."

Entering through the gate, Eli gasped in astonishment when he saw who was there. All around him were people who had died years ago! His mother and father wrapped their arms around him. His grandparents proudly watched him. Everywhere, family, friends, and the people he had ministered to on earth stood and applauded him, thanking him for all he had done for them and welcoming him home. Even Jesus' earthly dad, Joseph, was there, clapping his hands and smiling at Eli.

Tears of joy poured down Eli's face as he tried to take it all in. All these people were here to see him! Then he realized that even though they had once been sick, old, and weak, they now looked as beautiful, young, and strong as the angels.

"There is someone else who wants to see you," Naomi said.

Together, Rachael and Naomi took Eli, followed by his family, down one of the streets where they found another man who waited to see them.

"Eli, this is Father Abraham," Rachael introduced.

"Father Abraham!" Eli gasped. "I can't believe it's you. All my life I have read about you in the Scriptures. I have learned from your life and tried to live the life of faith and trust in God you showed."

"Welcome, my son," Abraham responded. "We have waited many years for the day when Jesus would go to the earth as the Messiah. We are now rejoicing that He is there. You taught Him the Scriptures as a child and cared for His family. You have done well. You were the first person, outside of His family, to see that He was the Messiah. You were the first person who trusted in Him. Your faith in Jesus has saved you and brought you here. Now you may rest here in peace with us until the day He returns.

As Eli and Rachael prepared to leave, Abraham smiled at him and placed his hand on his shoulder. "You must come by and we can talk sometime, yes?" "It would be an honor," Eli responded. "I would love to."

Eli looked around at the beauty and wonder of this place with its new smells and music and peace. He thought how much he would enjoy seeing his family join him there someday. Maybe he could introduce them to Abraham. As he turned to thank Rachael and Naomi for bringing him here he raised his eyes as if to ask what they would be doing next.

"So," Rachael said, smiling from ear to ear, "want to see more?"

"There's more?" Eli asked, surprised.

"Oh yes, there's more," Rachael responded. "You can't even imagine! Do you mind if Abraham joins us?"

Eli nodded enthusiastically as he left on his first tour of Paradise with Abraham, Rachael, and Naomi.

He wondered what lay ahead. Wouldn't that be a story?

12

Jesus Begins His Ministry

The sun slowly began its morning climb over the Judean Hills, causing long shadows to ease their way eastward across the red, pink, and brown soil toward the hills of Gilead. Along the Jordan River, green grass lined the banks as a wild-looking man in a heavy, rough coat sat there finishing his breakfast of grasshoppers and honey.

After breakfast, John, the son of Zacharias, stood and stretched his long frame. Tossing his coat aside he prepared for another day.

Soon, hundreds of people would be arriving from all over the country, drawn to him and his simple message, "Repent, for the kingdom of God is at hand."

And so it began. Like the waves of the sea they came. Hundreds of them were now arriving, asking the wild man if they could be baptized to show that they were truly sorry for their sins and were preparing for the coming of the long awaited Messiah.

The poor and the curious would come. The Roman soldiers would come to watch for any sign of trouble. The Pharisees and Sadducees would be there, not to repent, but to keep an eye on this "John the Baptizer." Not only was he annoying, they thought, he was also dangerous. They intended to check everything he said with the Scriptures so that they could accuse him of either making mistakes or simply being crazy.

As the people arrived from everywhere, John moved to the riverbank and began to speak the things that God had told him to say.

Raising his booming voice so that all could hear, he began. "Repent, for the kingdom of heaven is coming soon!" he boomed.

Then, looking at the Pharisees and knowing they were not even slightly sorry for their sins, he shouted, "You brood of snakes. Who warned you to try to escape from the judgment of God?"

Stunned by his words they blurted back, "Who are you anyway? Do you think you're the Messiah or something?"

"No, I am not," John replied.

"Are you Elijah, then?" they asked.

"No," John answered, "I am simply a voice in the wilderness warning you that the Lord is coming, and you need to be ready as the prophet Isaiah has said."

"So why are you baptizing people, then?"

"I baptize people with water," John replied, not answering their question, "but there is One coming after me who always existed and whose sandal strap I'm not worthy to untie. He will baptize you with the Holy Spirit."

Unable to understand what John was saying, they shrugged their shoulders and decided among themselves he was an insolent, mad fool. He was a popular mad fool, they thought, but that only made him all the more dangerous. He had a smart mouth too, talking to them like that! Someday, they vowed, they would shut that smart mouth of his. But for now he was too popular with the people. They would have to wait.

"He's eaten too many grasshoppers, and it's made him mad," one of them joked as they all laughed. So they sat down to watch as hundreds of people entered the water and were baptized in front of them.

Down into the water they went and then up again. The picture of baptism was a beautiful one. Being lowered into the water was a picture of dying or even drowning in their sins. Being lifted out was a picture of being washed free from those sins and rising again to live a new and better life. Over and over John baptized those who would come. Over and over the Pharisees and priests watched, not understanding that they needed this too.

When the sun set and the day was over, some people went home. Others stayed to see what the next day would bring. They had no idea that what they were about to see would change the world.

The next morning the sun rose just as it had the day before, and with it came the heat. Today the temperature would easily hit over one hundred degrees Fahrenheit in the shade, but there was no shade. As the people looked to the sky and found no clouds to block the heat, they knew they would have to endure it.

John had become such a "rock star" that this was the most important place to be in all of the country. No one wanted to miss what he would say next. The Pharisees and Sadducees were still there, waiting for any sign of trouble, as the people again began making their way to John to be baptized.

Suddenly John looked up and saw Him. From over the hill, Jesus appeared, approaching from the north country of Galilee and walking straight toward him.

Immediately John recognized his old Friend and Cousin from years ago. It was good to see Him again, but deep inside he knew this was no ordinary visit. No, this was not to talk about old times and to tell stories. There was purpose in Jesus' steps and John knew what it was. Jesus was about to begin His earthly ministry.

"I need you to baptize Me," Jesus said to His friend.

"Oh no, Jesus," John quickly protested. "Don't do this. I need to be baptized by you."

Softly Jesus replied, "No, John, this is the way it must be."

As hundreds of people watched, John gently lowered Jesus into the water of the Jordan River and lifted Him out again. As he did this, he found himself wondering why this was necessary. This was a baptism of repentance. As far as he knew, Jesus had never done a wrong thing in His whole life. What was going on here? Why was this necessary at all?

The moment Jesus was lifted out of the water it happened! God's Holy Spirit descended upon Him, appearing like a dove, and from somewhere in the sky a voice spoke that sounded like thunder. "This is My beloved Son, in whom I am well pleased."

In that moment John knew with absolute certainty that what the voice said was true! There could now be no doubt. His Cousin and old Friend from years ago was the promised Messiah the Jewish people had prayed would come. In that moment, John the Baptizer, the most important man in all of Israel, knew that the days of his importance were about to end. He had just baptized the Son of God. Jesus' time had finally come. The world would never be the same again.

Standing on the bank of the river with people lining up to be baptized, talk between Jesus and John about what had just happened could not last long. The time soon came when Jesus would have to leave, and John had work to do. As He turned to leave, Jesus hugged John and said goodbye.

"Where are you going now?" John asked his old Friend and Cousin.

"To the desert," Jesus replied. "I need to spend the next forty days there before I can eat again!"

13

The Desert

The desert is a wild and dangerous place to be, even when you have everything you need to survive in it. In the desert, days can become so hot that it feels as if the rocks themselves are melting before your eyes. In the desert, nights can be so bitterly cold that even surviving them becomes a nightmare of shivering and shaking.

In the desert, winds can blow sand at cruel speeds that can cut into a person's skin and blind their eyes. In the desert, sand dunes change with the wind and a person can become so lost they have no idea where they are or how to get home. Turning around and around, desperately trying to find their way out of the hot, drifting sand has even driven more than one person mad, causing them to collapse to their knees and give up hope.

In the desert, everything and everyone is always searching for food. You see, if you are not searching for food, food is searching for you, and dangerous animals are always hunting for something to eat.

But in the desert, the most desperate of all needs is water. There are ways to find it, of course, but if you can't find it, you will die. Yes, the land of sand is a very, very dangerous place to be. So, it was into this place that Jesus made His way after being baptized by John.

The number forty in the Bible is a number that speaks to us of testing, judgment, or learning through difficulty. For forty days, the flood waters of Noah's day poured down on the earth killing all who were not inside the ark God had told Noah to build.

For forty years, the Jewish people lived in the desert where they were tested, learning many lessons from God.

For forty days, Elijah went without food after his escape from an evil queen.

And so it was that now, in the desert, Jesus found the shelter and water that would keep Him alive for the next forty days. Here, He remained alone, preparing Himself for the years that lay ahead and the work that He had come to earth to do.

Here in the desert, having no earthly friends or family with him, yet not alone, He spoke regularly to His Heavenly Father, ensuring He learned how to recognize His Father's voice even when things were hard. He knew He needed to be able to hear and obey that voice in the heat, the cold, the sand, and the wind.

It was more important than food, so He did not eat. It was more important than comfort, so He did not quit and go home. It was more important than avoiding danger, so He trusted His Father to keep Him safe.

Hearing and obeying His Father would be the most important thing He must learn, and so He stayed. The sun burned and the winds blew. The sand hurt and the nights froze, but still He stayed. In Heaven He had always been God. On earth He was learning to be a man.

As the forty days came to an end, Jesus looked up to see a familiar face approaching.

"Surprised to see me?" Satan asked.

"No," Jesus replied, "not at all."

"I've come to make you an offer," Satan continued.

"I'm still not surprised," Jesus responded.

"Let's go on a little trip," Satan suggested. "I have some things I want to show you. By the way, You look hungry. If you're the Son of God, why don't You turn these stones into bread?"

But Jesus had learned to trust His Father to provide everything He needed, and magic tricks were not part of the plan.

"It is written," Jesus replied, "Man shall not live by bread alone, but by every word that proceeds from the mouth of God."

The "trip" Satan had in mind for Jesus took them to the Temple in Jerusalem. As Jesus stood at the highest point, far above the ground, Satan tossed out another suggestion. This time he used a little Scripture to back up his idea. "If You're the Son of God, throw Yourself down. It is written: 'He will send His angels to help you so you won't even stub your foot against a stone.'"

Throwing Himself off the temple and having angels catch Him and fly Him over Jerusalem would certainly get people's attention, but it was clearly not what His Father had sent Him to do. As Jesus listened to His Father's voice, He thought of a Scripture. "It is written that you shall not test the Lord your God."

Satan was getting desperate now. He needed Jesus to sin but he only had one idea left. Years ago in the Garden of Eden with Adam and Eve, it had only taken a piece of fruit to get them to cave in. Jesus was making it tough.

"Look," he began. "You see all these kingdoms in the world? You can have them! As a matter of fact, You can have them all if only You will fall down and worship me."

Satan was done. He had no more to offer. All he could do now was hope that Jesus would cave in and accept his offer.

Jesus' response came quickly. "Get away, Satan. It is written 'You shall worship the Lord your God, and Him only shall you serve.'"

Satan was furious but unable to do anything about it. He had just failed. Jesus had resisted him and every one of his temptations by simply quoting Scripture! Satan was beaten and embarrassed, and so, for now, he vanished.

By now, Jesus was extremely hungry and weak and exhausted. The time He had spent with Satan had worn Him down even more. But the forty days of testing were now over, and His Father quickly moved in to help.

Rachael, Naomi, Gideon, and other angels had been watching Jesus carefully for the last forty days and especially during this test with Satan. They had held their breath as Satan had tempted Jesus to have all the things He had a right to have, yet having to get them the wrong way. They prayed He would not fail but were not allowed to help. Jesus had to pass the test in His own strength and that of the Holy Spirit that now lived in Him. And He did.

Never since his fall from heaven had Satan been defeated like this. The angels cheered for this victory! Finally they were allowed to help Jesus and it did not take them long.

Rachael provided the food. Naomi gave Him a place to rest and a shelter from the heat. Gideon healed Jesus' cuts, bruises, and sunburned face. It felt like a reunion. It was almost like those days in heaven before He had become a man.

There in the desert they told Him how much they loved and missed Him. They served Him and they talked together again.

Rachael told Him about the things she had been doing and the families she had been protecting. She even mentioned Samuel and Rebecca and the things that had happened in their lives. It felt good to have this time together again.

But now it was time for Jesus to leave. He needed to return to Galilee.

14

Galilee

The rocks and clay made a soft crunching sound under His feet as the well-worn leather sandals continued their regular beat along the uneven road. Crunch, crunch, crunch, crunch. The only other sound was his strong, steady breathing that seemed to match about every fourth step or so.

Most people didn't notice Jesus as He walked north on the road to Galilee that day. Even those that did could not know where He was going or why He was going there.

But Jesus knew. Things were about to change in Israel.

As He passed the place where John was still baptizing people, He heard John's loud voice, speaking about Him to his followers. "Behold the Lamb of God who takes away the sin of the world."

Jesus smiled. John knew! And soon others would too.

Almost immediately, two men caught up to Him and began walking with Him. Andrew and John had just become the first two disciples that would travel with Jesus for the next three years!

Though they had been following John the Baptist, after hearing what John had just said, they knew they needed to follow Jesus now and learn from Him. They were not alone for long. Andrew was so impressed with Jesus that he immediately introduced his brother Peter to Him and he joined the small group too. By the next day, Philip and Nathanael also had been added, making them the first five men to become followers of the Carpenter from Nazareth. Together, they would learn and see things that the world had never experienced before. It would not take long. The teaching would begin when they arrived in Nazareth tomorrow.

It seemed that Mary knew and cared for everybody and that everybody knew and cared for her. Today she was on her way to Cana, just a few miles north of Nazareth. She had known Josiah his whole life, and though he was younger than Jesus, the two boys had played together as children and were still close friends. Because Josiah had always considered them friends, he had insisted that Mary, Jesus, and the whole family come to celebrate his special day with him. Today he was being married.

As Mary arrived, Jesus and His five new disciples were already there chatting with friends and family. Mary immediately realized there was a problem. Someone had miscounted the number of people who would be there at the wedding. They were running out of wine, and they were running out fast!

The servants were frantic and embarrassed at the error. To run out of wine at an event such as this would not only be embarrassing to Josiah, it would be considered an insult to the guests. This mistake would be remembered long after the wedding and could even affect how others treated Josiah. Instead of a wonderful day of celebration, this was now turning into a day of insult and shame that could haunt Josiah for the rest of his life.

Seeing Jesus, Mary immediately told Him the news. "They have run out of wine," she said.

"What does that have to do with Me?" Jesus asked. "My time has not come yet." Jesus had said this before when speaking to people. He had said it to His family. He had said it to Rabbi Eli, and He had said it to John. But now things had changed. He had been baptized by John and He had spent forty days in the desert. Though the full meaning of Jesus' words would not be completed yet, it was time for His ministry on earth to begin and He was ready.

Mary saw the twinkle in His eyes and the small smile on His lips that only a mother would notice and realized He knew just how important this was to His friend Josiah.

"Whatever He says, do it," she told the servants.

As all eyes turned to Him, Jesus spoke to the servants. "Fill any empty water containers with water," He said to them.

The servants found six huge, empty water containers. Each container would hold up to thirty gallons of water each. Quickly the servants began to fill the containers with water as Jesus had said.

"Now take some of the water and bring it to the party's organizer so that he can taste it," Jesus said, once the containers were full.

A servant scooped some of the water from the large container into a smaller one. Wondering why on earth he was doing this, he took it to the party's organizer to taste as Jesus had said. *Everyone knows what water tastes like*, he thought. *He's going to think we're crazy when he tastes this.*

As he poured the water into a drinking cup the servant gasped in amazement as he saw something he would never have expected. The water had changed color. It now looked just like, well, wine.

"This is unbelievable!" the party organizer exclaimed, as he tasted the sample he had just been given. Rushing to Josiah he could not hide his excitement. "Nobody ever does this!" he said. "Everybody hands out the best wine first, but you've saved the best for the last."

Though Josiah had no idea what had just happened, the servants knew. Jesus had changed ordinary water into enough wine, not only to save Josiah from shame but also to lift him up in the eyes of everyone at the wedding.

The changing of water to wine was the first miracle that Jesus would perform and only a few people would ever know how important this event was. From that day until the end of time, men, women, and children would be asked to place their trust in Jesus and to give Him control of their lives. When they did this, many would be laughed at and treated with shame and disgust. Jesus had sent a strong message. This first miracle would save Josiah from embarrassment and shame. In the same way, those who placed their trust in Him would never need to be ashamed.

15

Samuel and Rebecca

Rachael had watched as Jesus turned the water into wine in Cana, but now there were other things she needed to do. So she left for Bethlehem to see an old friend.

Thirty years ago, Samuel watched the night sky burst into light and the angels of God announce the birth of the Baby King in Bethlehem. He had been twelve years old then, yet he had never forgotten the thrill of seeing the angels, the light, and especially the small baby in the manger. The Messiah was born that night. He saw it! He had thought things would be different soon. Wouldn't the Messiah bring peace? But as to how and when things would change, he just didn't know.

He still remembered the horrible days that followed that night when Herod had ordered his solders to kill all the baby boys in the land. Almost everyone knew someone who lost a child because of that evil king and the Jewish people still hated Rome as much now as they had then. Surely the time for the Messiah to come was here! Even many of the priests thought so. Samuel knew what he had seen and believed the baby in the manger that night was indeed the Messiah, but nothing was changing, and Samuel just didn't know why. He was just a shepherd after all. He wasn't anybody important—at least to most people.

As far as Samuel knew, only two people in the world loved him. One person was his wife, Rebecca, and the other was his precious daughter, Miriam. It was not that people disliked him. Certainly not! Everyone who knew Samuel liked him. He was a respected shepherd now, and from time to time, he was put in charge of the famous Temple flocks. These were the lambs that the priests in the Temple used for sacrifice. However, as far as being truly loved by someone, Rebecca and Miriam were the only ones who did.

He had fallen in love with Rebecca when he first saw her. At first, of course, He had been attracted to her beauty. But as he began to spend more time with her, he grew to see that her beauty was just as much inside as well. Every time they talked together, he felt warm. He was fourteen then. She was a bit younger. Everybody knew they were meant for each other, and neither set of parents ever suggested that they even consider marrying anyone else.

He worked hard as a shepherd and people knew he was a man they could trust. He was honest and kind and giving, but his heart was always set on one thing, the day when he would be able to provide for Rebecca and finally become her husband.

Eventually that day came, and it was hard to know which of them was the most excited. Their special day was celebrated by friends that lived far and wide, from Bethlehem to Jerusalem.

Several important people came to town just to congratulate them and to wish them their best. One of these people was a man named Nicodemus. He was a very important Pharisee but was not at all like the others. He was kind and thoughtful and generous. Samuel had sold him some of his best lambs and Nicodemus had never forgotten him. For Nicodemus to remember Samuel and to walk all the way to Bethlehem for his wedding was a huge honor and it showed everyone the kind of man Nicodemus really was.

And so the wedding took place and Samuel and Rebecca finally became husband and wife.

Though they didn't know it, Rachael was there too, watching over them. Samuel had always been special to her and she wished he knew just how special all of Heaven thought he was.

At first, Samuel and Rebecca hoped they would be able to have many children, but it was not to be. Within a year, Rebecca became pregnant but lost the child within her first three months of pregnancy.

After that, nothing at all occurred for ten long years. Both of them had all but given up hope of ever having children though they still continued to pray that someday God would bless them with a child of their own to love.

Finally, the day came when Rebecca knew it had actually happened. She was pregnant again. God had heard their prayers and she was going to have a baby. She and Samuel actually danced for joy in their small house.

When it was time for the baby to be born, Rebecca's labor was hard; both for her, the midwife, and Samuel, who waited outside. When it was finally over, both Rebecca and her new daughter were fine, and Samuel knew he had never seen such a beautiful baby girl. They named her Miriam, after Moses' sister, and she immediately became the most important thing in her parents' lives. They were careful not to spoil her as she began to grow and because of this, she became a kind and gracious child. Her soft heart always led her to consider others before herself, and as a result, she was loved by all who knew her.

The evening was cool and in the stable, chores were being completed. Samuel had just finished milking a cow when Miriam, who had been playing by herself in the hay, ran over to be with her dad. Just as she passed behind the stall door, the cow backed into it and knocked the unlocked door into the child. The force of the door pushed her back, her hands flying into a burning lamp on a shelf. Immediately the lamp fell into the hay, setting the stable and Miriam ablaze with fire!

Samuel heard the screams and leapt to his feet to run to his child, grabbing a jar of water as he went. After throwing the water on Miriam to extinguish the fire, he scooped her up and rushed out of the stable screaming for Rebecca to come and help.

As Rebecca came from the house, she saw Samuel carrying their daughter.

"The lamp fell into the hay," he called. "See if she's OK while I try to get the animals out and save the stable."

Miriam is kicked into the lamp.

Rebecca saw that Miriam was hurt, but all she could do was hold her daughter and try to comfort her while Samuel worked to free the animals. When the neighbors came to help, the animals were rescued and the fire was put out, but little Miriam had been badly hurt from being trapped in the burning hay.

As the days and weeks passed, Samuel knew that Miriam would recover, but she would not escape the damage the fire had caused. The burns had left a huge scar covering over half of her face, and her left arm was paralyzed by the damage the fire had done to the muscles there.

She was still the same sweet Miriam, but she no longer had the same beautiful face that Samuel loved to hold and kiss. Gone as well was her ability to play the way she had loved to do before the accident.

Day and night, Samuel felt haunted by the feeling of guilt for not stopping the fire. In his mind, he had failed to protect his daughter. Though Rebecca tried to comfort him, he knew the horrible truth. It was all his fault.

Rachael was there during the accident, but this time God didn't allow her to stop it. She had helped as the fire was put out. She had helped as Miriam slowly healed. She had seen all of the support for the family that poured in, but she had not been able to stop the fire.

Even though Rachael knew that God loved Samuel and Rebecca and Miriam, she still felt sad for them, and she hated not knowing why this horrible thing had happened.

Today, six years after the horrible fire, Rachael flew to Bethlehem and stopped at Samuel's home. She saw Samuel working across the field with his sheep, his face still marked with sadness. She could see Rebecca working around the home. Although she looked tired from the troubles she had endured, she still looked as lovely as the day she had married.

Miriam, on the other hand, broke Rachael's heart. The girl was twelve years old now. She still had a kind and warm personality. As Miriam helped her mom as much as she could, Rachael saw her scarred face and the left arm that hung helplessly by her side. Her physical wounds looked like they had healed as much as they could on the outside, however, the scars and disabilities remained.

Rachael longed to be more of a help to this grieving family, but she knew she couldn't make all that pain go away. So she watched and she just felt sad.

16

The Galilean Ministry Begins

Word had spread about the wine thing. In a small town when something happens, people talk about it, and everyone was talking about Jesus changing water into wine at the wedding. *We had better keep an eye on this guy,* everyone was thinking. So Jesus began to attract all kinds of attention, both good and bad. On the good side, many people now listened to Him and seriously thought about the things He was saying and doing. On the bad side, a growing number of people decided that no matter what He did, they would be against it.

In His hometown of Nazareth, Jesus was asked to read from the book of Isaiah. Standing in the synagogue He read, "The Spirit of the Lord is upon Me, because He has anointed Me to preach the gospel to the poor; He has sent Me to heal the brokenhearted, to proclaim liberty to the captives and recovery of sight to the blind, To set at liberty those who are oppressed; To proclaim the acceptable year of the Lord." Looking up, He closed the book, saying, "Today this Scripture is fulfilled in your hearing."

Many people were shocked to hear Jesus say that this Scripture, which obviously referred to the Messiah, was actually about Him. By the time He finished reading, the people were so angry they dragged Him to the side of a cliff and were going to push Him off. But as they argued among themselves, Jesus simply walked away.

Shocked, they stood there and tried to think of what to do next.

Meanwhile, Jesus had places to go. First on His list was Capernaum.

At the synagogue in Capernaum, the people listened and were amazed as Jesus taught them as no teacher they had ever heard before. Though they did not know it at the time, long ago He had been the writer of the very Scripture He was now teaching. No wonder He taught it so well and with such authority.

Suddenly a man with a demon inside him blurted out in a loud voice that was not really his own, "Let us alone. What have we to do with You, Jesus of Nazareth? Did You come to destroy us? I know who You are; the Holy One of God."

"Be quiet and come out of him," Jesus ordered the demon, who was actually one of Satan's fallen angels.

Throwing the poor man to the floor, the demon shook him one last time, came out of him, and left. Amazed, the people stared in wonder, asking a question that people would ask for the next two thousand years. "Who is this man who can cast out demons with a simple command?"

Leaving the synagogue, Jesus now headed to Peter's home to have lunch and to rest. Here, Peter's mother-in-law was sick with a fever.

Having a fever today is not very serious. You usually feel rotten and miserable, but you get better. However, two thousand years ago, having a fever was a very big deal. The problem was that with no prescription drugs or hospitals, like there are today, you didn't know if you would ever get better. Often when a person had a fever, it was the beginning of something terrible, maybe even a plague, for the whole community.

Even knowing all this, this was the house Jesus headed to for rest. Entering the home, He went to the poor woman's side, stood over her and simply commanded the fever to leave. As everyone watched, the fever left her body, and she became completely well! Immediately she got up from her bed and began serving them lunch. Amazingly, after all she had been through, she was not even tired.

Again, news spread like wildfire that a man was in Peter's house who could heal the sick. By evening, they began arriving from everywhere. The sick and the demon possessed all arrived at once with one simple hope, that this Man of God would heal them. And He did.

One by one, every sick person who was brought to Him was healed, and every demon was cast out. As His fame began to spread far and wide, it was not long before the chief priests in Jerusalem began hearing stories about Him. These were the men who were in charge of the Jewish people during this time when Rome ruled over Israel, and now they too began wondering the same thing as everyone else: "Who is this man?"

Because this question needed to be answered quickly, they began sending out spies to get some answers. Unfortunately, behind their open interest in Jesus lay a more sinister and evil motive, they did not just want answers, they wanted the answers they wanted. And so, as they gathered together to discuss this Jesus of Nazareth, they came to a decision. If this Jesus from Nazareth was going to become a problem for them, well, they would just have to do something about it, wouldn't they? After all, they had ways of dealing with troublemakers.

Nicodemus rose from his sleep and began to prepare himself for another day. Today he would learn more about this carpenter from Nazareth who had the other Pharisees so upset. He would listen to reports from eyewitnesses who saw the things Jesus had done and then he would tell the other leaders what he had found out. If they didn't like what he said about Jesus, they could do what they wanted. However, he wanted to know the truth. Jesus fascinated him. Who was He anyway?

By the end of the day, Nicodemus felt his head was going to explode. Listening to all of the stories about what Jesus had done was forcing him to completely change his thinking. The things that He was doing were, well, let's face it, impossible. Yet there were so many people who had seen them happen with their own eyes that he could not ignore them or call them crazy. Deaf people now heard. Blind people now saw. The sick were healed. The demons were being cast out. Who was this man? Whoever He was, Nicodemus thought He had to be from God if He was doing all of these things.

Then Nicodemus, the Pharisee in charge of finding out about Jesus, got the most interesting news of all. The next day, Jesus of Nazareth was going to be in Jerusalem for Passover, and Nicodemus knew exactly where He would be.

The day certainly did not go as he expected. Jesus showed up early, went to the Temple, and immediately started causing trouble. Making a small whip, He headed straight for the moneychangers. Because travelers from faraway lands needed their money changed so they could buy lambs to sacrifice, the moneychangers were making themselves rich by charging massive fees for simply exchanging their money. Now, using the small whip He had made, Jesus forced them to leave the Temple area, spilling their money onto the ground and turning over their tables after them. But it was what He said next that got their attention. "Do not make My Father's house a house of merchandise."

Who does He think He is? Is He saying that God is His Father? thought the chief priests. *That is illegal.*

They had had enough. When they questioned Jesus about it, He simply told them, "Destroy this Temple and in three days I will raise it up!" This answer nearly drove them crazy.

"It's taken forty-six years to build this Temple, and You're going to rebuild it in three days?" they exclaimed, astonished. Yet, they didn't understand what He was saying and that when He used the word "Temple," He was talking about His own body.

Jesus left the Temple in a storm of confusion and controversy. The chief priests wanted to get rid of Him right away, but many people followed to find out more about Him and who He was. The sick found Him too, and He healed them just as He had done in Galilee.

17

The Night that Changed Everything

Nicodemus had tossed and turned all night trying to at least get some sleep. He needed to be rested in order to think clearly when he finally met with Jesus tonight, but his mind would just not let him relax! *Just how should I handle this situation?* he wondered.

He couldn't tell the other Pharisees about the meeting because He really wanted to ask Jesus honest questions about who He was. He knew they would not like this idea and that no matter what he told them, they had their own plans for Jesus anyway. In short, it would be very dangerous to go against their plans. No, this would definitely have to be kept a secret. There was no other way around it. He would tell his wife, but that would be all.

Finally the time had come and Nicodemus crept out of the dark night shadows to finally approach Jesus face to face. He knew what had happened earlier that day and in a way it made sense to him. The moneychangers had practically taken over the Temple area and were charging people from other countries outrageous prices to change their money to the currency used there or to buy animals for sacrifice.

It had happened slowly, over time, but now everyone had become used to it. Maybe they should have done something about it long ago, but now most of the priests got a portion of this money for allowing it to go on. They would never agree to change things now.

Unlike his fellow Pharisees, who tended to be proud bullies, Nicodemus was a polite gentleman. So it was that he finally approached the man he had waited so long to meet.

"Shalom, Rabbi," he said with respect.

"Shalom, Teacher," Jesus replied, also showing respect, but also letting Nicodemus know He knew exactly who he was. "It's good to see you tonight."

"Rabbi, we know that You are a teacher who has come from God, for no one can do these signs that You do unless God is with him."

If Nicodemus had complimented anyone else in this way, he would have expected to see pride on that person's face; to his amazement, Jesus didn't even respond to what he had just said.

"Truly, I say to you, unless one is born again, he cannot see the kingdom of God."

Nicodemus had not expected Jesus to say anything like this and struggled to find an answer! The only thing he could think of was a question.

"How can a man be born when he is old? Can he enter his mother's womb again and be born?"

Jesus' response was immediate. "Truly I say to you, unless one is born of water and the Spirit, he cannot enter the kingdom of God. What is flesh is flesh, and that which is born of the Spirit is spirit. Don't be surprised that I say this. You must be born again."

Nicodemus was the most famous teacher in the entire land of Israel, but he had no idea what this meant! Jesus looked him in the eye and told him something he knew he needed to know, but he couldn't understand it. He felt like a brand new student who knew nothing.

"How can these things be?" he asked simply.

Jesus looked at him with understanding and sadness.

"Are you the teacher of Israel and do not know these things?"

As Jesus continued to speak to him, Nicodemus listened for whatever he could catch and understand. Jesus assured him that He knew that everything He was saying was true, though many, especially the chief priests and Pharisees, would never believe. He stated that He knew who He was and from where He had come.

Jesus then said something that Nicodemus could at least partly understand. "As Moses lifted up the serpent in the wilderness, even so must the Son of Man be lifted up, that whosoever believes in Him should not perish but have eternal life."

Nicodemus had no trouble remembering the Scripture that Jesus was speaking about. During the time the Jewish people had spent wandering in the wilderness, they had been disobedient to God, who had punished them by sending poisonous serpents into their camp. Even though God was using the serpents to punish His people, He had instructed Moses to create a serpent made of bronze and place it on a high pole. Everyone who had been bitten by the serpents was simply told to look at the serpent on the pole, then the miracle would happen. Whoever looked at the serpent, being held high in the air over the camp, was immediately healed from the burning, poisonous wounds of their snakebites.

But Nicodemus was still confused. *What does this have to do with me?* he wondered.

Jesus then said what would become the most famous words in the entire Bible. "For God so loved the world that He gave His only begotten Son, that whoever believes in Him should not perish but have everlasting life."

Nicodemus continued to listen to Jesus teach in a way that he had never seen before. Never in his life had he heard anyone speak with such authority, but it was hard to understand some of the things He said.

Soon the teaching time was over, and Nicodemus left for home. *What was it that Jesus was trying to teach him?* He wondered.

18

The Search

"Born again," Jesus had said. What did that mean? It was so confusing, yet somehow, as Nicodemus struggled to understand the things Jesus had told him, he knew it was actually simple. He just had to see it.

Now, as the things that Jesus said to him swirled around inside his head, Nicodemus needed to be alone so he could try to make sense of them. He knew he had been taught something important, but what? Finding a time and place to be alone was not going to be easy, especially today. He had so much to do.

He had his report to finish for the High Priest about what he thought of Jesus. He would have to be careful there. If he said anything good about Jesus at all, the High Priest would be furious.

He was also expecting some Passover lambs from his shepherd friend from Bethlehem today. Yes, it would be good to see Samuel again. *I wonder how he's doing?* he thought to himself. Nicodemus headed north along the main street of Jerusalem, called the Cardo, meaning 'the heart', then turning right just past the Temple, he made his way through the growing crowds toward the Sheep Gate. This is where he planned to meet Samuel, who would have his lambs.

As he drew near to the famous old Sheep Gate, it looked and sounded like a zoo rather than the magnificent Temple of the Living God! Sheep, lambs, goats, birds, oxen, and cattle filled the streets and holding stalls that lined the area. Over the chatter and yelling of the people, the bleating of sheep and the mooing of cattle filled his ears—not to mention the smell. He was definitely in the right place. Then, looking straight ahead, he saw Samuel waiting for him.

"How are you, my friend?" Nicodemus called as he approached Samuel, stretching his arms out for a friendly hug.

"I'm well, Teacher," Samuel replied as he hugged the big man.

He really appreciated Nicodemus. Nicodemus was the only Pharisee he could think of who would openly be friends with a simple shepherd like him.

"It's so good to see you again, Samuel. How long has it been? Wasn't it last Passover?"

"I think you're right, Teacher," Samuel nodded. "It has been too long. Maybe you have found someone else to get your lambs from, eh?" he joked.

Nicodemus laughed. "No, no, my friend. Never. Who else in Israel would sell me such fine lambs for such a price?" It felt good to laugh again with this man.

"So how is Rebecca and that little girl of yours?"

"Rebecca is well," Samuel replied. "Miriam is growing up so quickly I don't know if you would recognize her if you saw her now. She still has pain and the scars, but she never complains. She's a good girl."

Nicodemus could see the pain in Samuel's eyes. "I wish I could help her," he said softly.

"You have done more than enough already," Samuel replied. "You hired doctors I could never have paid for. She is alive! I can't thank you enough."

Nicodemus paid Samuel for the lambs and turned to leave when, suddenly, a thought came to him that completely surprised him! He had been constantly thinking about the things Jesus had said the night before and had just remembered something.

Jesus had said something about the serpent that Moses had lifted up. When the children of Israel were in the wilderness and sinned against God, He, in turn, had brought a plague of "fiery" serpents to bite them because of their sin. However, because of His compassion and mercy, God told Moses to make a "fiery," bronze serpent, instructing him to put the serpent on a pole and then to hold up the pole. When he did this, the people who looked at the bronze serpent were healed from their snake bites.

To make the serpent, Moses had to put bronze metal into the fire and melt it down so it could be formed into what God wanted. Six years ago, Miriam had fallen into a fire. She had grown into an amazing and godly young girl, but she still had those awful scars.

"Samuel," Nicodemus called out to his friend.

Samuel turned and made his way back to the teacher.

Nicodemus thought carefully about how he should say this. "There is someone I would like you to meet." Being careful not to say anything about the night meeting they had had, Nicodemus began telling Samuel the things he knew about Jesus. He told him about the wisdom he had seen in Jesus' eyes and heard from His lips. He told him about the sick people Jesus healed by touching them or with His words.

"Can I introduce you to Him?" Nicodemus asked.

Samuel listened carefully but tried not to hope too much. What if this was all a mistake? What if only more heartache and disappointment lay around the corner? How could he get his hopes up only to see them dashed again? How would this hurt Rebecca?

Nicodemus saw his hesitation and fear. "I don't know, Samuel," he said, "but I believe this man, and I know He would not hurt you or Miriam or Rebecca. I have reliable reports that He has already healed many people and done amazing things. Look, the other Pharisees hate Him, so He can't be all that bad, eh?"

Samuel smiled. "OK," he said. "Where is He?"

"I don't know Samuel, but I'll find out. You go and get Miriam and Rebecca and we'll find Him together."

As Samuel left to travel the five miles back to Bethlehem, he wondered if he was doing the right thing. What would Rebecca think? Would she think he had lost his mind and gone chasing after dreams that could never come true?

He would tell her about his talk with Nicodemus and what he had said. Hopefully she would understand. He felt guilty and responsible for what had happened. If there was any hope left in the world, he wanted to reach for it.

The talk with Rebecca seemed to go well. Like Samuel, she didn't want to get their hopes up only to have them dashed again. They had all been through so much. But Rebecca loved Samuel more than he would ever know, and after all these years, she knew that he still blamed himself for Miriam's terrible accident. If this were going to be a way for Samuel to finally find some peace, she would not stand in the way.

So she hugged him, told him she loved him and respected his decision, and said she thought this was a great chance for Miriam. But inside, she was scared to death.

Meanwhile, Nicodemus asked every person he knew where Jesus would be that evening; but this time, no one seemed to know. Jesus had spent Passover in Jerusalem with His disciples, but after that, no one appeared to know where He would be next. Everyone's best guess was that He would be near the Mount of Olives.

That evening, Samuel arrived at Nicodemus' door with Rebecca and Miriam by his side. Miriam had not been told why they had brought her here, but Nicodemus could see in Rebecca's eyes how frightened she was that this might only cause more pain.

"Let's go and see if we can find Jesus," Nicodemus suggested. So together they left for the Mount of Olives. Finding Jesus was the only hope they had left for their daughter's healing.

Nestled snugly in the Mount of Olives overlooking Jerusalem was a garden where Jesus and His disciples often prayed. Here it was that as the sun slowly slipped below the horizon, Samuel, Rebecca, Miriam, and Nicodemus began their search for the Carpenter from Nazareth whom some were beginning to call the Messiah.

Crossing a brook called Kidron, they slowly climbed a hill and entered the garden through a small gate. Standing at the entrance, they searched the garden for any sign of Jesus or His disciples. But Jesus was nowhere to be seen. The garden was empty.

The feeling of dissapointment hit them like a wave of the ocean crashing on the shore. They had missed Him and had no idea where He now was. Their only hope seemed to have been snatched away.

19

The Touch

As they made their way back down the hill in the dark toward Jerusalem, even Miriam sensed the sadness that had descended upon her family and their friend. Though she still did not know exactly why her parents wanted to meet Jesus of Nazareth, she knew that it was important to them. Even though she too felt disappointed, she tried to encourage them anyway.

"Don't worry, Abba," (which means daddy), she pleaded in an attempt to cheer him up. "If God wants us to find Jesus, He will show us the way."

Samuel and Rebecca smiled at their daughter proudly. They realized she was right. They had let their disappointment drown their faith. They were looking for Jesus, a Man of God. Couldn't He take care of them, even now?

Nicodemus stared at the girl in amazement. He had not seen such faith even in the house of the High Priest.

"Look, why don't you all stay at my home tonight?" Nicodemus offered. "The road back to Bethlehem can be dangerous. Tomorrow is a new day. Maybe God will show us what to do."

Samuel and Rebecca looked at each other, nodded, and thanked Nicodemus for his offer. To stay at the home of such an important man was a great honor. Maybe tomorrow would bring better news. If anybody could find Jesus, Nicodemus could.

With the first rays of sunlight peeking over the Judean hills, Jesus and His disciples were already well on their way into northern Judea. Normally the trip back to Galilee would take them east of the Jordan

River and on up the well-traveled path there. Had they been taking this route, they would have spent the night in the Garden of Gethsemane on the Mount of Olives. However, Jesus had other plans. He needed to go into Judea.

There, the disciples would baptize those who decided to follow Jesus; after that, they would walk home to Galilee through Samaria. Jerusalem was only a few hours away from the place where Jesus and His disciples would be teaching and baptizing. Because of this, it did not take long for news to travel back to Jerusalem that the teacher from Nazareth was in Judea, openly teaching and baptizing.

Fortunately, that news quickly reached Nicodemus before Samuel, Rebecca, and Miriam left for home. This time they knew where Jesus was.

After the disappointment of the night before, hope again returned when they heard this exciting news. Quickly getting their things together, they again left Jerusalem, this time heading north into the Judean countryside to find Jesus.

Samuel had never told anyone except his closest family and friends about seeing the angels and the baby in the manger when he was a boy. Early on he had discovered that when you told someone such things it usually changed the way people thought of you. Mostly they thought you were crazy.

Rebecca, of course, had never thought he was crazy. She had always believed him, yet she understood how he felt and agreed with Samuel about keeping it a secret. It was a secret they had kept until now.

"Nicodemus, how old do you think Jesus is now?" Samuel asked as they walked along the road.

"Oh, I don't know. He should be about thirty or so, I would think," he replied. "Why?"

"Because I saw something thirty years ago that you should know about," Samuel replied.

So as Nicodemus listened with his mouth open in astonishment, Samuel told his friend the story of the most amazing event in his life.

"Do you know what this means?" Nicodemus asked.

"I think I do," Samuel replied.

"If we are correct, and Jesus was actually the baby in the manger, there can be no doubt that He is the promised Messiah."

They walked along in silence as Nicodemus thought about what he had heard. *How should I handle this information?* he wondered. Who would believe it? The Pharisees would never change their minds. They already hated Jesus and nothing he said would change that. He had been put in charge of finding out about Jesus, yet he realized that if he spoke the truth about what he had found out, it might place him and his family in real danger. What should he do? He decided that he would wait and see for now.

They heard the noise of the crowd before they saw anything. Crossing over the crest of a hill, they saw at least five hundred people below. As they drew closer, they saw a couple of the disciples baptizing people in the river while Jesus taught others on the edge of a small hill. Nicodemus, who had already met Jesus a few nights before, recognized Him first.

"There He is!" he exclaimed.

Miriam, who saw how relieved everyone was to have found Jesus, burst out with a delighted "Mama, Abba, we found Him. We found Him! I knew we would!"

Samuel took a deep breath. They had finally found Jesus. But would it do any good? There had been so many disappointments in the past. Would this be any different?

All eyes turned to Nicodemus as he moved closer to the people gathered below. Everybody knew he was a priest and a Pharisee, and most people knew that he was the most respected teacher in Israel. *Why would he be here?* they wondered.

But no sooner had the people begun to wonder about Nicodemus than all of the attention shifted to a young girl who stood close behind him.

The veil that Miriam often wore in public had been left at home in the quick rush to leave on their journey, so now she stood there with nothing to hide her scars and injuries. Her right hand jerked up in an effort to try to cover her face, but it didn't work! As soon as people saw her, they automatically stared at the scars and began whispering.

Her shiny skin started high in her scalp, where no hair would grow, and went down across her almost-closed left eye and swollen lips. Her left arm hung limply and even her hand showed evidence of the awful burns she had endured. Miriam knew what it felt like to have people stare at her, but it still hurt. She was twelve now and knew exactly how she looked to others. At home, people had become used to her looks, but here she stood out even in a crowd. Shy and embarrassed, she had learned to keep her head down so most people couldn't see. However, in a place like this, hiding her face wouldn't work. Everybody had already seen all they needed to see. So she bravely stood there as people stared at her and whispered among themselves.

As they made their way down the hill, Jesus looked up at them and smiled at Nicodemus, waving at him to come over. When Nicodemus arrived at His side, Jesus looked into his eyes and asked, "Have you learned yet what it means to be born again, Nicodemus?"

Nicodemus, who had still had very little time to figure it out for himself, quietly shook his head.

"It's what happens when you search for Me with all your heart," Jesus responded. "But it appears you have now found Me, haven't you?"

Yes I have, Nicodemus thought, *I have indeed.*

Turning to Samuel and his family, Jesus said, "It's good to see you, Samuel."

"How do You know my name?" Samuel exclaimed, astonished.

"You were among the first to greet Me when I came into this world," Jesus replied. "Thank you. Your visit meant a lot to my mother."

Samuel and Rebecca stood amazed in front of this man who seemed to know everything about them, but Jesus now turned to Miriam.

As He looked at her and smiled, Miriam realized that He knew her too. He knew everything about her! He knew what she had gone through and every tear she had cried. He understood her pain and fear and embarrassment. He didn't see her as a disfigured, crippled person. He saw her for who she really was. He saw her hopes and dreams. He had heard all of her prayers and for the first time since she could remember, she felt peace.

"Come here, little one," Jesus spoke to her as He gently took her in His arms.

Invisible to humans, Rachael gasped as she remembered the promise Jesus had made to her in Heaven before He had even come to earth. He had said exactly those words to her. He had also promised that when He did, He would think of her.

As Miriam sat on His knee, Jesus placed His left hand gently on her face while holding her limp left arm in His other hand. "You loved and obeyed your parents and encouraged them to come to Me," Jesus said to her. "You felt I could heal their pain and never thought of yourself. Go in peace, little one. Your faith has saved and healed you."

Miriam felt a small tingle run down her arm. This was the first feeling she could remember having that was not painful! She looked down, shocked that she could now move it freely and easily, as if it had never been hurt at all.

She hadn't felt anything happen to her face, but all around, people gasped in astonishment at the change that happened. The burned skin that had covered her face simply crumpled away and fell to the ground leaving behind new fresh skin that was as soft and smooth as when she was a baby.

"She is beautiful!" people cried.

"He healed her face!" others were saying.

As she began to understand what had happened, Miriam turned to her mother and father. Both of them now exploded into tears as they looked at the beautiful, new face of their beloved daughter, now smiling for the first time in six years. Miriam watched as Rebecca turned to Jesus with her face flooded in tears and her voice choking out the words, "Oh thank you, thank you, thank you!"

Samuel had fallen to his knees, trembling before Jesus, unable to think of a single thing to say except, "Thank you, Master!" His eyes, filled with tears, said it all in a way that words never could.

Nicodemus stood in silence and watched. He knew that because of all the things that had happened that day, his life would never be the same. Never in his life could he have expected to see such things as he had just seen.

As they all moved away and let others approach Jesus, they saw Him glance at them one more time. This time He paused for a moment, smiled, looked at Samuel, Rebecca, and Miriam together and said, "Oh by the way, I know an angel who is particularly fond of you! She says hello."

Rachael could not believe her ears. In the middle of all this, Jesus had remembered! As He had picked up Miriam He had thought of her, just as He had promised at the Great Palace.

Rachael had always wondered why God had not let her stop Miriam from being burned. Maybe she would never know. But she did realize that if that had never happened, what had just taken place would have never occurred.

To be loved and wanted and needed by others is a very special thing. Some people go their whole lives without ever knowing how special they really are!

Samuel had never thought he deserved to be loved, especially after Miriam's accident. Now he saw the truth! God deeply loved and wanted him! After all that had happened, he knew God had forgiven him and had set him free to start over again.

He looked at Rebecca, who still sobbed with tears of joy running down her cheeks. He saw Miriam, now laughing with newfound joy, and both hands touching her new face again and again.

As he watched them, he knew they were now free too. After all, isn't that what real healing does?

20

The Tour

The tour of Paradise was more than Eli could have ever imagined. Rolling hills, green pastures, rivers of clear, pure water, birds, and animals were everywhere. People were everywhere too—thousands upon thousands of them who had lived from the time of Adam until now. It was amazing that even though there were so many people here, it didn't seem crowded at all.

It's a well-known fact that whenever people get together on earth, they usually make a mess. The larger the town or the city is, the larger the mess is. But not here! When Eli looked around, he could not see a single thing out of place.

There was no litter or pollution. The sky was clear and blue. There was no scorching from the sun to burn him. As a matter of fact, though there was light all around him, he could not see if there even was a sun.

The sounds of soft music filled his ears. He couldn't tell whether it came from voices or instruments or maybe even both. It didn't interfere or distract him. It was just there! Beautiful and peaceful, it was everywhere.

"It's wonderful, isn't it?" Abraham asked.

"I can't believe it," Eli responded, still staring at his new surroundings.

"I knew Paradise would be, well, Paradise. But I think that with all the distractions that I faced on earth, I never really gave it much thought. I guess I was too busy doing other things. After all, I had a synagogue to manage and people that needed me."

Rachael now spoke. "We know you were busy, Eli. And because of that, you need to see something else." Abraham nodded his head because he knew what was coming.

"It's time to see the reason you worked as hard as you did, Eli," Rachael suggested softly.

As soon as she had said that, a new sight appeared before their eyes. Gazing ahead, Eli now found himself in a peaceful garden, surrounded by flowers and trees. Before him, a huge canyon now appeared, which no one could cross.

As he looked across the gigantic gap, dark clouds of smoke rose into the air, rolling in the sky and blocking the light from reaching the land. Looking carefully, Eli could see the cause of the smoke. Small flames licked the ground and scorched everything in sight until it became a sooty, black, greasy mess.

Rachael explained, "This is Sheol, the place of torment. Those who refuse to believe they need a Savior will come here. They will be held here until the Day of Judgment. That is why you worked as hard as you did, Eli. Because of what you did with your life, many people will not have to come here."

For the first time since arriving in Paradise, Eli stared at Sheol in shock and horror. He never could have imagined such a place. Never had he understood that the consequences of not believing in a Savior would be like this.

Abraham stood beside him and stared across the canyon. "We all know people who are over there in Sheol, Eli. We tried to warn them, but they refused to listen."

Rachael knew what Eli was thinking. "God *is* fair Eli," she said. "No matter how it looks, He did everything He could to get them to listen! Even now, Jesus is working on earth to make a new way for every person to be with Him forever."

As they were talking, Abraham noticed a young man approaching them. "Lazarus," Abraham exclaimed as the two men hugged each other! "How are you my friend?"

"Better than I was on earth," Lazarus responded with a wide smile.

Turning to Eli, Abraham introduced Lazarus to him. "Eli, this is Lazarus. He came to us a short while ago. He used to live close to where you lived in Nazareth."

"Yes, I remember you!" Eli exclaimed. "You became sick and had to beg for food when you had no family to help you."

"That's right," Lazarus replied. "I knew where your synagogue was, Rabbi, but I became too sick to get help. When I finally died, these two angels brought me here," he said, pointing to Rachael and Naomi.

With Lazarus and Abraham resting and talking on the grass, Rachael continued to tell Eli more about Paradise. They took their time. There was no rush to get home. They were now in eternity.

A voice calling from across the great gulf broke up their time together. "Father Abraham, Father Abraham," the voice cried. Everyone saw the man frantically calling out from the smoke, flames, and filth. "Father Abraham, please send Lazarus over here that he might dip his finger in water to cool my tongue. I'm so thirsty in all these flames."

Sadly, Abraham replied, "Don't you remember, son, that while you lived a life of luxury on earth you never bothered to lift a finger to help Lazarus, who was dying just outside your door? Now you want him to comfort you? Anyway, it's impossible for anyone to cross this gulf."

For a brief moment, the man on the other side thought about what Abraham had said. He realized it was true. No one could get across that huge gulf. He would never find anyone to help him. "Father Abraham," he called back in desperation. "If he can't come here, please send him to my father's house. I have five brothers who need to be warned so they won't have to come to this place."

Abraham replied, "They have Moses and the prophets' writings. Your brothers can read them."

"They won't do that," he replied. "But if someone comes back to life from the dead and goes to them, they'll repent."

Softly, Abraham answered for the last time, "If they did not believe Moses and the prophets, they won't believe even if someone comes to them from the dead."

With that, the discussion was over. No one could help the man on the other side, and Lazarus would not be warning anyone by going to them from the dead. The time for making decisions about eternity is while you are still alive.

As Eli sat with Abraham, Lazarus, and the two angels, he realized how important it was to carefully think about where you wanted to go after your life on earth. He had decided as a young boy to follow God. Later on, he recognized Jesus as the Messiah when he saw Him.

Lazarus, though he was extremely poor and dying in poverty and disease, still put his faith and trust in his God. Abraham, though he had sometimes made mistakes, had been an example of how to trust God during times of trouble more than any other person in history.

Across the canyon, however, there were many people who had not chosen so wisely. Other things had seemed more important in their lives on earth. For them, God could wait. And now they were there.

Eli didn't want to end his first day in Paradise here at the canyon's edge. He was thankful, though, as he remembered all the people he had encouraged to trust God with their lives. Preparing to leave, Eli rose; and turning his back on the smoky canyon, his eyes again scanned this amazing place he would now call home. Looking around, the beauty of heaven seemed to make all those efforts on earth worthwhile.

Eli was relieved that the tour of Paradise had continued once again. With Rachael and Abraham guiding him, Eli began to meet many people along the way. He met Adam and Eve, the first man and woman, who now lived in a garden without sin. He met Moses and Joshua in the city where they now lived. Samson and Gideon greeted them as they walked down one of the streets. Elijah waved at them from a small hill as they passed by. Ruth smiled and waved at them. Even Queen Esther knew his name and welcomed him to Paradise.

It seemed that there was no end to the wonder of finally being here in this amazing place. Eli wondered if eternity itself would be enough time to meet and share and learn from all these wonderful people.

At the end of the tour on that incredible first day, Abraham finally returned home. Now it was time for Rachael to show Eli his own new home. Seeing it for the first time, he was amazed that this place had been prepared for him. As he looked around, it appeared to him as though his home had been made to meet every need he would ever have. The thing that attracted him most to this place was not its size, like some of the mansions on earth, but it was everything he could ever have wanted. It was comfortable, clean, and warm. It contained everything he needed. It felt good. It felt peaceful. It felt like a place he would enjoy sharing with others.

As he expressed this to Rachael, her response shocked him. "You won't be staying here for long, Eli," Rachael told him. "The time is soon coming when everyone will move."

"What?" Eli asked, astonished. "Why?"

"Because things are not yet finished," she replied. "The next place will be better."

PART 3

The Journey Home to the Great Palace Begins

21

The Sychar Connection

The long walk back to Jerusalem went quickly. At times, everyone was quiet. Then suddenly, the whole story would spill out again like a huge jar of water poured out onto the ground, with everyone talking about the miracle. Again and again they would look over at Miriam just to see if it was real, and there she was, still feeling her face and looking at her hands. It was real! She had been healed in a moment by Rabbi Jesus from Nazareth—the same person Samuel had last seen as a tiny baby in a Bethlehem manger over thirty years ago.

They could hardly wait for the moment when they would arrive home and their friends would see for themselves what had happened. The closer they got to home, the more excited they grew. What an amazing story they had to tell!

Although Nicodemus was not the most talkative man in Israel, he too was caught up in the excitement, chattering with Samuel and Rebecca as if he were a small child. "Such a gift!" he would say. "Look at her! Such a gift. I can't believe it!"

Now, as he walked quietly, his thoughts returned to the future and what all of this would mean. What should he say to the Pharisees? How should he respond when they asked him what he thought of Jesus? And here was the big one: who did *he* think Jesus was? Did he have the courage to tell them the truth? If he did, it would not only put his own life and those of his family in danger but also the lives of Samuel, Rebecca, and Miriam. He would need wisdom to handle this. He would need to be very wise indeed.

Samaria was a place where most Jews never wanted to go. The people there were not even true Jews anymore. Hundreds of years ago, they had married people who were not Jews from other countries and started their own culture and traditions. They didn't follow Jewish traditions anymore like the rest of the Jewish people. They had drifted so far away from the teachings of the Scriptures that all of the other Jews thought they were the lowest, filthiest people on earth.

And so it was that while Nicodemus, Samuel, Rebecca, and Miriam traveled home to Jerusalem and Bethlehem, Jesus and His disciples walked north through Samaria to a town called Sychar. Although the disciples didn't know it yet, Jesus did; another woman's life was about to change forever.

The woman's name was Abigail, which meant, "My father is joy." But for Abigail, joy, much like her father, was something she didn't have in her life. Oh, how she wished she could go back in time and change those silly years when she had carelessly chased after boys who only saw her as a thing to play with but cared nothing at all about how she felt or who she was.

During those years, she had broken her father's heart. Night after night, her mother had cried herself to sleep. They had fought and shouted and argued, until finally, one day she left home.

At first she had felt free. Free to do what she wanted and to go out with whomever she wished. But it did not last. Eventually, her boyfriend would leave her. Then she would find someone else to go out with, and then another, until finally she would be unable to remember who she really was.

Now she could not see any way out of the disgrace and shame she had brought upon herself and her family. She knew she had made terrible mistakes, but now the other women would not even talk to her. What she had once thought was freedom had now become a dark, lonely prison.

Today she was gathering water from the public well in the heat of the day, and she was alone because the other women were too embarrassed to be seen with her. How had it come to this? If only she could go home again! But that could never happen now.

A man's voice broke the silence and shook her from her thoughts. "Could you give me a drink?" He asked.

Looking over, Abigail saw a stranger sitting near the well. He looked tired and thirsty. He also looked like a Jew. *What's He doing asking me for water?* she wondered. Well, at least He was talking to her. He obviously didn't know who she was.

"How is it that You, a Jew, are asking me, a Samaritan woman, for a drink?" she asked.

His reply sounded like a puzzle. He was obviously playing with her, she thought, but at least they were still talking. "If you knew the gift of God, and who it is that is asking you for a drink, you would be asking Him for living water and He would give it to you," He replied.

Abigail completely misunderstood the words Jesus had just used when He said He would give her living water. Living water is a picture of the Holy Spirit who would be given to every person who trusted Him. Here Jesus was saying that just as cool water refreshes the body, so the Holy Spirit will refresh and give life to anyone who would trust Him for eternal life.

Thinking instead that Jesus was offering her well water, Abigail had another question. "But You have nothing to draw water with and the well is deep. Where are You going to get this living water? Do You think You are greater than Jacob, who gave us our well?"

The Stranger responded, "Whoever drinks from this well will be thirsty again, but whoever drinks from the water that I give will never thirst again. It will spring up in them like a fountain of everlasting life."

Abigail looked at the stranger. He was not flirting with her as so many other men had. He was kind and sincere. This man meant what He was saying. Whatever this living water was, she knew she needed it.

As she thought about everything a woman had to do to get water from a deep well, she replied, "OK, Sir, give me this water so that I will not become thirsty again or have to come all the way out here to get it."

The Stranger's reply stung. "First, go and get your husband and bring him back here with you."

"I don't have a husband," she replied.

"That's true, you don't," the Stranger answered. "You have had five husbands and the man you are living with now is not your husband."

Ouch! She didn't want to talk about this. What could she say? Who was this man that He could know these things about her?

"I think You are a prophet," she said.

This was getting uncomfortable. *I know, I'll change the subject to religion,* she thought to herself, looking at Mount Gerizim in the distance.

She pointed to the mountain shimmering in the heat. "Our fathers worshiped on this mountain and you Jews say that Jerusalem is where a person needs to worship."

The Stranger responded with an answer that would shake her, for He spoke with an authority she had never heard before. His words seemed to grab at her lonely heart and point her to what was real and true and important.

"Woman, trust Me, the hour is coming when you will neither worship on this mountain nor in Jerusalem. You have no idea what you worship because salvation comes from the Jews. But the hour is coming and is already here when true worshipers will worship the Father in spirit and in truth. These are the people He is looking for. God is Spirit, and those who worship Him must worship Him in spirit and in truth."

Abigail thought for a second. It was hard to have someone tell her the truth about herself because she had made so many bad choices in her life. It was not easy for her to be honest. Maybe she should end their conversation now.

"Messiah is coming," she said quietly, "the one called Christ. He will tell us all things."

And then the Stranger shocked her with seven small words that would forever change her life. "I who speak to you am He."

As other men joined the Stranger, Abigail slipped away. She did not hear what they were talking about. She didn't even want to know. She had no doubt in her mind that she had just met the Messiah, the Christ. Now she had to tell someone.

At first, she told the man with whom she was now living and to her surprise he actually listened. He too was shocked that a Jew they had never met could know these things about them. Her news about Jesus spread quickly as more and more people heard about it—even the elders of the city.

"He said to come see Him," she said to the people now listening to her story. "He's at the well now! Let's go."

As Jesus was teaching His disciples, He lifted up His head and saw Abigail coming with a large crowd. "The fields are already white for harvest!" He said, looking at the white robes worn by many of the people coming to the well.

As the disciples watched, they too saw the huge number of people making their way toward them at the well. Most of the people were men. However, Abigail was in front of them all, leading the way. For the first time she could remember, she was smiling.

Jesus stayed two days with them in Samaria. He taught, listened, and answered the people's questions. He taught them about how far they had drifted away from God's will, but He also showed them how much they were loved in spite of their sin.

Looking across at Abigail, Jesus spoke about how people's pasts could turn them into slaves. Often, they would start off by making a few bad decisions and the next thing they knew, they were trapped in sin with all the pain and suffering it could bring. Yet, through it all, He also spoke about how repentance and forgiveness could set even the most lost sinners free. Samaria had sinned greatly against God, but Jesus Himself told them how He deeply desired to see them free and serving God again. He, the Messiah, would forgive them if they would only ask. And many did.

Two days later, Jesus again returned to Cana of Galilee, where He had changed the water to wine. Not surprisingly, the news about His arrival spread quickly. The miracle with the wine had become a huge story here and not a single person had forgotten what He had done.

Suddenly an important nobleman from Capernaum pushed his way in front of Jesus. "Please, Master, my son is dying and he needs Your help! Even now he is at Capernaum in bed struggling for breath. Please come before he dies."

Jesus' reply was not what the man could possibly have expected. "Go your way; your son lives."

The nobleman froze for a moment as his mind raced. *What? You won't come? You say my son is now OK? How do You know? If I leave, what will I do if there is no change and my son never gets well? If I stay and beg, I will insult the very Master I am asking for help.*

Slowly, he came to the only decision he felt he could. Deciding to believe what Jesus said was true, he thanked Jesus, turned and left for home. The slow, downhill trip home took several hours, but it seemed like days. His mind swirled over and over as he thought about what had just happened. Wondering if he had done the right thing, his doubt fought with his faith. Belief fought with unbelief, but he kept walking, wondering if his son was alive or dead.

As he descended the steep hills to Capernaum, his servants were already running toward him, waving their hands wildly and shouting. Lifting his eyes, he saw them in the distance. *What could this mean?* he wondered. *Has my son died already and I wasn't there when he needed me the most? But surely this is not the way they would tell me he had died.* They looked like they had good news.

"Your son lives!" they shouted. "Your son lives!"

Running toward them, hugging them, and dancing with joy, he could hardly control his emotions. Breathlessly he asked them the first question that had just entered his mind, "When did my son get well?" The servants' answer stopped him in his tracks. His son had been healed at the same moment Jesus had told him his son would live.

Less than fifty miles away to the south, a man jumped to his feet as his wife screamed, shooting her hand toward her mouth to cover the sound. Though they had both heard the knock, it was she who had answered the door. Racing to her side, he reached out to steady her before she could fall. Only then did he turn to see the person who was standing outside. With his whole body trembling, his eyes filled with tears at a sight he had been certain he would never see again.

"I'm so sorry," the young woman kept saying as tears poured down her wet cheeks.

With cries and sobs and tears filling the air, the man and his wife flung their arms around the daughter they had not seen in over fifteen years. The anger, shame, and bitterness of the past faded like a morning mist into the warm sunshine of forgiveness, love, and overwhelming joy. Abigail had come home.

22

The Galilee Controversy

The tour of Paradise was now over. Eli had settled into his home when Rachael received her new instructions. Naomi and Gideon were already at the Jordan River when Rachael swooped in at maximum angel speed, (something like a hummingbird staking its claim on the largest flower in the garden). She arrived so quickly they both nearly jumped out of their wings in surprise.

Rachael could tell that Gideon was upset as he quickly updated her on the problem that was unfolding before them. Roman soldiers were, even now, on their way to where John the Baptist was baptizing and they were not coming to repent of their sins.

"Remember how we dealt with Belial and Nahash?" Gideon asked. "We could do something like that again." Both he and Naomi now had their swords drawn and were ready for battle. If they appeared as Roman soldiers, they could easily defeat the real soldiers that were now arriving from Jerusalem.

"No!" said Rachael. "Our instructions are clear. We are not here to stop the soldiers. We are only supposed to make sure that the people are not hurt."

"But they are going to take John away!" Naomi exclaimed.

"I know, but God is allowing it to happen. Just make sure the children don't get in the way or get hurt."

As the angels watched, the soldiers approached the river and called to John. "John the Baptizer!" shouted the soldier in charge. "In the name of King Herod, we are placing you under arrest. Come with us and no one will be harmed."

As John looked at the soldiers standing on the bank of the river with their swords drawn, he knew that his time as the great preacher in Israel was over. He knew when he baptized Jesus that this would eventually happen, and now the time had arrived.

"Don't hurt anybody," John called out. "I will go with you wherever you wish."

With this, he climbed out of the water, turned to the people who were watching, and asked them again to repent of their sins. "There is one coming after me who is now here," John cried out. "I am not worthy to untie His sandal. Hear Him."

As Rachael and the angels watched, John stood before the soldiers, smiled at them, and said softly, "I'm ready. Let's go."

There was no need to tie his hands or bind his arms. He wouldn't cause any trouble. So John the Baptist, the man who was once the most important preacher and prophet in Israel, was led away down the bank of the Jordan River, along the eastern shore of the Dead Sea, and to a prison in a castle known as Machaerus.

Though the Pharisees and many other rulers were beside themselves with excitement and joy over the arrest of John, the Jordan was just not the same anymore without his huge, booming voice crying out for people to prepare the way for the Lord.

With John's arrest, Jesus now became the focus of attention and as all eyes turned to Him; people began to wonder what He would do now. "Is He really the Messiah that John spoke about?" they asked each other. They would soon see.

Over the next months, Jesus spent most of his time around Capernaum, on the northern shore of the Sea of Galilee, and He was now busier than ever. People continued to come and to hear Him teach, but the miracles were what really caught everyone's attention.

Leprosy was a horrible disease. It was a disease that made it necessary for anyone who had it, even children, to leave home and live in a special place with other lepers. The moment a person came down with this disease they were considered dirty. They could not even be touched by those who were not lepers themselves. These were the people who came to Jesus for help. They had nothing left, and Jesus healed them and made them clean.

Imagine what it would be like if you couldn't walk, run, or even feed yourself. Imagine being blind, unable to see anything that was going on around you. Imagine being deaf, unable to hear a laugh or a cry or to even know what others were saying. Imagine what it would be like if you couldn't speak or tell another person how you felt. These are the people who came to Jesus. These are the people He healed and made well.

Jesus was kind to those who had never heard a kind word. He spoke the truth to all who would listen, and it drove the Pharisees crazy.

Today, as Jesus taught at a home in Capernaum, a growing noise interrupted the lesson. Outside, some men had brought a paralyzed friend to the house, hoping maybe Jesus would heal him. Seeing how large the crowd was and realizing they would never be able to get

Cutting through the roof.

through all of the people, they quickly came up with a brilliant plan. Why not break through the roof of the house?

Climbing onto the roof and dragging their friend with them, they began digging a hole until it was just big enough. Then, carefully, they lowered their friend through the roof into the house and onto the floor below, just in front of where Jesus stood. That got everyone's attention.

Jesus smiled as He watched what was happening and almost laughed at the sight. A young man now lay in front of him on a bed with four ropes tied to it that led up to the hole in the roof where four heads peeked through. He resisted the temptation to thank the man for dropping in to see Him.

Waiting a moment for things to calm down, and knowing how much it meant to this man and his friends for him to be here, Jesus looked at the man and said something completely unexpected. "Young man, your sins are forgiven."

The Pharisees immediately went volcanic. Like a mountain exploding in fire, they just couldn't stop themselves. "What! Who does He think He is? Doesn't He know that only God can forgive sins? Blasphemy!" they screamed.

Jesus waited for them to calm down enough to listen and then began to speak. "Why are you thinking this way?" He asked. "Look, what do you think is easier to say, 'Your sins are forgiven you,' or 'Rise up and walk'?"

The Pharisees were trapped. Obviously, only God could heal someone and only God could take away his sins. If Jesus healed this paralyzed roof-crasher how could they then say He couldn't forgive him? So they waited nervously, secretly hoping that the man lying in front of them would remain paralyzed. But that wasn't going to happen this day.

Loudly and clearly and in front of everyone there, Jesus said to them, "So that you may know that I can indeed forgive sins, look closely."

Turning to the man, He simply said, "I say to you, arise, take up your bed and go to your home."

You could almost hear the Pharisees groan as the young man began to move. Rising to his feet he began praising God and thanking Jesus for giving him back his life. Tears flowed down his cheeks. Never would he have expected this. "Thank You" seemed too small a thing to say, but what else could he do?

He could tell people what had happened. He could stand and walk and jump and move. Then a thought struck him. If he was indeed healed, and he obviously was, his sins had been forgiven as well.

His sins were forgiven! He was free to live the life God had created him to live. So as he and his friends left the house, he decided that this was exactly what he would do.

Now more disciples joined the small group of men following Jesus. There was John and his brother James. Both of them had now left their fishing business so they could be with Jesus wherever He went. Another disciple was Matthew, a tax collector for the Romans. Matthew had been hated by the Romans because he was a Jew, yet the Jews hated him just as much because he worked for the Romans. There was no place for him to live in peace until Jesus came along. So when Jesus looked at him and said, "Follow Me," he immediately stopped being a tax collector and never once looked back. He felt this was the best decision he had ever made in his life.

But now a cloud was forming over Galilee that would seriously darken the days that lay ahead. It was not the type of cloud that held rain or hid the sun, but it would make its presence felt, and it was definitely going to produce a storm.

It began at the synagogue in Capernaum where Jesus frequently went to pray and to teach. As He entered the synagogue, He immediately noticed a man with a withered hand. Growing up, this man had been bullied and teased by the other children and their cruel jokes. Now he continued to suffer the pain and frustration of trying to do even the simplest tasks.

But today was the Sabbath. The Pharisees had come up with a whole list of things that people were not supposed to do on that day and it didn't take them long to notice Jesus when He came in.

Immediately they began to watch Him to see what He might do. They had not forgotten how He had healed the paralyzed man the other day or how He insulted them by claiming to forgive the man's sins after they had said He had no right.

They watched Him closely, their faces angry and hateful. *Don't even think of healing this guy on the Sabbath*, they thought.

Looking at them and knowing what they were thinking, Jesus turned to the man who needed healing and said, "Step forward." Now, turning to the Pharisees he asked, "Is it lawful to do good or evil on the Sabbath? To save life or to kill it?" Again, they had no answer.

Turning to the man again, He said, "Stretch out your hand." As soon as he did, his hand was restored to perfect condition, just like the other.

The Pharisees said nothing, fuming with anger at this Man who was making them look foolish by asking them questions they could not answer. Who did He think He was, causing trouble like this? He would pay for this. They would make sure of it. So, as they left the synagogue, they began to make plans. As soon as they could, they would kill Him.

23

Bethesda: A Place of Waiting

Caleb dragged himself along the filthy street as he slowly, very slowly, pulled himself toward the place where he was going. The people who passed him on the way had seen him before but did not slow down to become involved with his problems. These days they had enough of their own.

He had been to this place before, often. For thirty-eight years now he had been coming here, hoping to be made well. But it had not happened. He was still partially paralyzed, lame, and very tired. He was always tired.

Sometimes, someone would help him, but not often. He now spent his days begging for food and lying by the pool. Every day he thought, *Maybe today*. But in thirty-eight years, nothing had happened. He was still lame and dirty and tired. Why didn't God just let him die? Surely that would be better than this.

Finally, arriving at the pool he laid out his blanket and slid onto it, slowly settling into his place. It was always the same place.

It was known as the Pool of Bethesda and strange things happened there! Every once in a while an angel would stir up the water in the pool. When this happened, the first person who got into the water was healed. It didn't matter what was wrong with them.

Many times, with his own eyes, Caleb had watched as people had been healed as they slid into the pool. But it was never him. He could never make it into the pool in time! He was too tired, he was too slow, and he was too sick.

Where is God for me? he wondered.

He looked at the water. Nothing was happening. There would probably be no angel visiting here today. He wondered why he even bothered to come. He was so tired.

Rachael watched as Caleb settled into his place by the pool. She had often seen him there when she had come to stir the water. Many times she had watched with delight as people were healed but had always felt sorry for Caleb, who could never make it in time. Sometimes she wondered, as Caleb had for so long, why God allowed this continue.

Today she would not be stirring the water. Today people would look longingly for even a ripple to appear, but the water would remain still. But that did not mean nothing would happen. No, something was going to happen, all right, and she was going to be there to see it.

As you look at a map of Galilee and Jerusalem, you will see that Jerusalem is at the bottom while Galilee, with its towns of Nazareth and Capernaum, is at the top. Because of this, it's easy to think that a trip from Galilee to Jerusalem would be going downhill. But, suprisingly, this is not true because Jerusalem is on a hill. Approaching Jerusalem, even from a distance, travelers would be able to see the Great Temple on this hill called the Temple Mount. So it is, that whenever people go to Jerusalem—and it never matters which direction they come from—they must first travel the large hills outside the city, climbing up to get there.

This year at Passover, Jesus and His disciples, now twelve in number, again made the long trip from Galilee *up* to Jerusalem. There were several people living in and around Jerusalem that Jesus would enjoy visiting again. He would love to see Nicodemus and find out how he was doing. Maybe He would even visit Samuel and his family. But today, He had another appointment.

Entering Jerusalem through the Sheep Gate He passed by the porches, or beautiful enterance areas, and entered the Pool of Bethesda. Looking down almost under His feet, a very sick man lay not far from the water's edge. The man's eyes were closed and he had that hopeless look on his face that Jesus had seen all too often.

Jesus knew exactly why the man was here. It was certainly no secret what happened here from time to time. The man was waiting to be healed, but it was clearly impossible for him to get himself to the water in time. He would be here a long time trying to get into the water as soon as the angel stirred it up.

Jesus of course knew all this. He knew exactly who the man was and how long he had been waiting. Jesus was around thirty-two years old now Himself, and this man began waiting here six years before Jesus was even born.

"Do you want to be made well?" The question Jesus asked seemed almost silly.

Of course I want to be made well. What do you think I'm lying here for? For thirty-eight years I have thought of nothing else! The last thing I need is You, the perfect picture of health, to stand here and insult me with stupid questions.

Caleb could have said all of these things to the man standing before him, but he did not. Obviously, the man was a stranger and didn't know how things worked here. There was no need to insult Him back with a smart mouth. So Caleb simply replied with the truth, "Sir, I have no man to put me into the pool when the water is stirred up; while I'm trying to move, someone else always makes it in before me."

In a strange way, Jesus' question did not seem stupid at all. Did he really want to be made well? He had never really thought of it that way before. *Of course he wanted to be well,* but was he ready for what that change would mean? He would have to change his entire life. He would have to work. He could no longer just beg. What would he do? What would he like to do? The questions hung in his mind for a while.

Yes, Caleb thought, he wanted to be well. But how was that going to happen? All the problems with getting into that water were still there. No one knew when the angel would come, and certainly no one would stand back and wait for him to slide and crawl his way to the water's edge.

If you were to ask Caleb what happened next, he would be able to tell you every detail. The things that happened in the next few moments were fixed into his memory as clearly as if they had been recorded. The Stranger, in a voice that was soft yet firm, spoke the words that Caleb would remember for the rest of his life. "Rise, take up your bed, and walk."

That's all the man said. There were no trumpets. There was no applause from heaven. Just those words.

A tingle passed through Caleb's entire body. He didn't feel any pain, just that small tingle. It almost tickled him. Then it was gone. With one breath, he had been tired and struggling for air, and with the next, he was healthy.

He looked up at the Stranger who was smiling at him. The man had told him to do something. What had it been? Oh yes. Now he remembered. The man told him to pick up his bed.

Caleb reached down and picked up his filthy blanket. He had rested on it every day to take the pressure off his sores. The sores. Where were they? Gone, of course! He was well!

Looking at the man, Caleb nodded his thanks. What could he say to thank this man for this gift He had just been given? "Thank You" seemed too small. He felt like shouting, crying, and even dancing. He could do it now. He knew he could. He even had the energy.

Even though it seemed too small, Caleb said, "Thank You. Thank You for giving me my life." Then, with his bed in hand and a spring in his step, he walked away.

Rachael hung on her wings and watched as Caleb walked away. As she looked over at Jesus, she saw that He was still smiling. He knew that Caleb's life would be very different now. Thirty-eight years ago this sickness had left him paralyzed. It had changed his life forever. Now he had a second chance.

Jesus, however, had just made a choice that would drag Him into a battle He did not want, yet it was one that He needed to fight and win. He looked up in Rachael's direction. She knew He saw her.

Things were about to change. Today was the Sabbath. Of all the days this could have happened. There was no question what that meant.

As Caleb returned home, it didn't take long for him to run into a group of Pharisees.

"What do you think you're doing?" they asked.

"Going home," Caleb replied.

"You're carrying your bed, you fool. Don't you know that's against the law?"

"Listen, you know I have been paralyzed for years. A man just healed me and told me to pick up my bed and walk home. I'm just doing what He told me to do."

"What man?" they asked.

"I don't know," Caleb replied. "I don't know who the man was."

"If you ever find out, let us know," one of them replied. "We would like to meet this man someday." Now, with their conversation finished, Caleb continued home.

Caleb hadn't been able to go up to the Temple since he had become paralyzed. The steps had been too high and difficult for him to climb. But not now. Now he would make his way to the Temple to properly thank God for healing him. After he had offered his sacrifice and given thanks, Jesus found him again. Caleb saw Him coming toward him and smiled widely as He approached.

"Thank You so much for what You have done for me," he offered.

Jesus' response surprised him and turned his thoughts again to the paralyzing sickness he had had for so long. "See, you have been made well. Sin no more, lest a worse thing come upon you."

Caleb nodded in agreement. He would live a much different life now than the one he had lived before. Thirty-eight years as a paralyzed beggar has a way of changing you.

After spending about an hour talking and listening to Jesus, the time finally came to go home. Leaving the Temple, Caleb passed one of the two Pharisees he had seen earlier. "If you still want to meet the man who healed me, He is over there," he told them.

As they looked over and saw Jesus standing there, the whole picture suddenly came together for them. This was the man who had turned over the tables in the Temple. This was the man who had caused all that trouble in Galilee. This was the man who had said He was going to destroy and rebuild the Temple in three days. Just who did this Galilean think He was? He had no idea who He was dealing with here. The last thing they needed was for people to start following this man who didn't even know how to behave on the Sabbath. This would stop, and it would stop now. The Pharisees in Galilee had already started planning how they would kill Jesus. Now the Pharisees in Jerusalem would begin to plan the very same thing, and they were even more dangerous.

24

A Time for Learning

It was exciting to see people who had suffered for so long being healed. Thousands of people came, not only to be healed themselves but to simply watch these amazing events.

Miracles like this were extremely rare in Israel. Yes, there had been miracles during the time of Moses; but by the time Joshua had died, very few were happening at all. There had been a rash of miracles during the time of Elijah, but within a generation, they too had all but disappeared. These amazing events were called miracles because they didn't happen very often. One might say that miracles were events that were scientifically impossible but happened anyway.

But the other interesting thing about miracles was that they almost always told a story! They meant more than they appeared to mean, and people needed to be taught to see.

During the time of Moses, God used the plagues of Egypt, like the millions of frogs that appeared, to show people His power, not only over the land but also over the gods that the Egyptian people worshiped. When Moses stretched his rod over the sea and split it in two, leaving dry ground for the children of Israel to escape on, God was saying, "I can always give you a way to escape, even if it seems impossible. Trust Me."

When God provided the Jewish people with bread from heaven, or manna, He was saying, "I can feed you. Trust Me." When God made water pour out of a desert rock, He was saying, "I can refresh your lives and not let you die of thirst. Trust Me."

And so it was, when Jesus performed His miracles, He wanted people not only to see what He was doing but also to understand what He was saying. Turning water into wine became a picture of the improved quality of life only He could provide. It stood for a life of honor and value that would never bring shame.

Just as wine or grape juice is deeper and richer than water, so a life spent following Jesus becomes deeper and richer than simply living any way we wish. Jesus, therefore, is Master over quality.

Casting out demons clearly demonstrated Jesus was Master over Satan. Healing Peter's mother-in-law showed that Jesus was Master over sickness. Healing leprosy not only showed how Jesus loved those whom the world had thrown away, it showed His power to make them whole again. Jesus, therefore, was the Master of restoration. Healing the nobleman's son, who was over twenty miles away, showed that it never matters how far away you are. Jesus is Master over distance. Caleb had waited thirty-eight years to be healed. Jesus is Master over time. Other miracles had their meanings too. The people just needed to look and see.

Now, leaving Jerusalem, Jesus again returned to Galilee. He had some teaching to do. Sitting on a hillside, which sloped down to the shining Sea of Galilee, He taught His disciples important lessons they would need to know.

This time of teaching, known as the Beatitudes began with teaching these men, as well as others that were there, about how God saw people. First, He taught them that it was what people were like on the inside that was most important.

He also taught them that, unlike here on earth, poor people and those who were suffering were valuable to God. Those who wanted to follow Jesus should not puff themselves up and "trash talk" others. Anyone who followed Jesus must also want to do the right thing and to be a good example to others. This is known as being righteous.

Next, Jesus taught about being merciful to others. This would mean not always judging people when they made mistakes. He told those who were listening to be honest. They also needed to be peaceful, even when they were tired, rather than bugging others and creating trouble.

These things would not be easy and often those who tried to live this way would be picked on and hated themselves. When this happens, Jesus taught, "Do not worry. Rejoice, for God knows that you're trying to do what's right and will reward you in your real home called Heaven." Over and over, Jesus said that those who did these things would be "blessed," a word that means *deeply enriched*.

As the lessons continued, Jesus told His disciples that He was actually fulfilling the Law of Moses. This series of laws included hundreds of rules that God had given to the Jewish people. The list covered what God wanted from His people. But it was so complicated and difficult that no one alive has ever been able to actually obey it.

Even wishing you could break the Law was wrong. That meant that every person in the world had broken God's Law. Every person, that is, except Jesus. He would be the first person in history to never make a mistake.

He taught His disciples how much God loved His people, even those who had made many mistakes. He taught them that no one was innocent before God, no matter how good they thought they were. If He, the Messiah, loved these people, then His disciples needed to love them as well.

Then He taught them how to talk with God. As they sat on the hill, Jesus taught them that talking with God should not be hard and complicated. It should be easy, like talking to another person. They should ask for things that they needed but must be careful not to become greedy. They should allow God to work out His plan for things, rather than insisting that things go their way.

Jesus also warned that not everyone who claims to be His follower actually is. He said that a day would come when God would judge each person for what he or she has done, but that those who truly love Jesus and the things He taught would be safe.

Anyone who has ever gone to school knows that learning can be long, tiring, and difficult. Sometimes it's exciting to learn new things. Sometimes it's hard to put together lessons taught by a teacher and apply them to things that happen in real life. Jesus knew this as He led His disciples down the mountain. If they were going to be able to trust Him, they needed to see that He was who He claimed to be.

Once they reached the bottom of the mountain, Jesus was again surrounded by people who needed His help. A leper approached Him asking Him if He was willing to make him clean. Jesus replied, "I am willing, be cleansed." Immediately the leprosy vanished!

A Roman centurion came forward who had a dying servant. Even though Jesus agreed to come and heal the boy, the centurion said, "Lord, I am not worthy that You should come under my roof. Only speak a word and my servant will be healed." Amazed that this Roman believed so strongly in Him, Jesus healed his servant on the spot.

Rachael had been there on the hill, watching as Jesus taught His disciples. During that time, she had been nodding her head in agreement. If only humans could understand these things, what a big difference it would make in the world, she thought.

As she watched over some children who were playing close to the water's edge, she listened to the Roman centurion asking Jesus to heal his servant boy. She knew the boy and just how sick he had been.

As Jesus told the centurion his servant had been healed, Rachael quickly zipped over to their home. Just as Jesus promised, the boy who had been paralyzed with fever and had been near death suddenly relaxed. His breathing returned to normal. The fever, which had been burning him up, simply vanished. The boy was healed. His mother, who only moments ago had been certain that her son was going to die, burst into tears of joy as she wrapped her arms around him.

Rachael loved this part. This kind of good news was all too rare these days. It was amazing to see, even for an angel.

The disciples were getting used to seeing Him heal the sick. They had seen it so many times. Jesus had even healed Peter's mother-in-law, but as yet they were still missing the real point. Yes, they still thought it was cool and enjoyed the show; but until now, they did not really see themselves as being the sick ones in need. They needed to experience a miracle that would impact their own lives. One was coming, and it was much closer than any of them thought.

25

Questions, Answers, and Storms

Another night had finally passed. The rats had scurried away into whatever holes they called home, and John the Baptist stretched his long body out as far as he could to get rid of the cramps in his body. He had never lived a life of luxury and even though his cell was small, hard, cold, and full of rats, his situation could have been worse. Herod fed him and even allowed visitors. There had even been times when Herod wanted to talk to him.

John had never changed his story in front of the king. Herod had married Herodias, his brother Philip's wife. That was just wrong and John had told him so. The king needed to repent like everyone else.

The lock on his cell door rattled. As the door was opened, two of his disciples stood there. These men were his good friends and had faithfully visited him since he was taken to prison, months ago.

"How are you, John?" they asked as they sat on the floor next to him.

"Oh, I'm fine," John replied. "Missing my grasshoppers and honey though," he added, jokingly.

They smiled, nodded, and told him what had been happening in the world since he had been put in the Machaerus prison. As John listened, he wondered if he had made a mistake about Jesus. He had always felt, as had many others, that when the Messiah came, the world would become a better place and there would be a time of peace. But that was not happening. The Romans were still in charge of their land. Herod was still Herod. The poor were still poor. The

Pharisees still didn't care. How could the Messiah be here and not fix all of this?

As his friends prepared to leave, John asked them to do him a favor. "Go find Jesus, will you? And when you find Him, ask Him if He is really the Messiah." Nodding their agreement, the disciples of John the Baptist agreed to find Jesus of Nazareth. They needed to ask Him a question.

When her husband had died several years ago, she had done everything she could to continue raising her son. She had worked hard, and even though they didn't have much, they had survived. As soon as her son was old enough, he too went to work. It was the only way they could make enough money to buy food.

The government certainly wasn't going to help. The very idea of getting anything from Herod was silly. So they both worked hard, and they both stayed alive, until the sickness came.

With her son ill she tried everything she could to help him, but slowly, day after day, he became sicker and sicker, until yesterday. Yesterday her son died.

After all she had been through, it had now come to this. Not only had she lost her husband, but now her son had died as well. Just as they had been doing better in their life, death had ripped her son from her. Now she was alone—alone to care for herself, to find work, to find food, and alone to grieve for her son.

She was getting older now and less able to do hard work. After all this she would probably have to beg for food. Even after all she had been through, she wasn't really angry; she was just broken. She was tired and defeated, without enough energy to know what to do next.

They were carrying her son's body through the streets of Nain to the place where he would be buried when Jesus saw her.

Nobody ran up to Him and demanded He do something. It was too late. The boy was dead. Everyone knew you couldn't change that. Everyone but Jesus.

As He caught her eye, He spoke to her. "Do not weep." Then turning to the open coffin and stopping those who were carrying it, He touched it and said, "Young man, I say to you, arise."

As all who were there watched with surprise and shock, the young man sat up and began to speak. No one heard the words he spoke because everyone's eyes were now on Jesus. He was smiling as He turned to the mother, who had collapsed to the ground shrieking with joy.

Helping the young man out of the coffin, He gave him to his mother. Throwing her arms around Jesus she sobbed uncontrollably, thanking Him again and again and again.

Her life had been given back to her. Her son was alive. She would not have to beg in disgrace! God had not abandoned her at all.

The people of Nain stared back, amazed and afraid at what they had just seen. *Who was this man?* "God has visited His people," they said. As Jesus turned north to leave and head back to the Sea of Galilee they could not know how right they were.

The men found Jesus on his way back to the Sea of Galilee and ran to catch up with Him. "We are from John," they explained. "He wants to know if You are the Messiah, or should we look for someone else?" Looking at them for a moment, Jesus decided not to answer their question right away. He simply beckoned them to follow.

Never far away were the people. Always the people. Always the sick. Always the needy. Jesus stopped, and as the disciples watched, the people approached with their needs. Although Jesus' disciples had seen Him heal people many times, John's disciples had never seen anything like it.

Jesus healed person after person before their eyes. The blind, the lame, the lepers, and the deaf were healed, and it did not take long for them to hear about what had just happened in Nain.

Jesus now turned to John's disciples and gave them a message for John. "Go and tell John the things you have seen and heard: that the blind see, the lame walk, the lepers are cleansed, the deaf hear, the dead are raised and the poor have the gospel preached to them."

John would understand this message. Years ago, David, Isaiah, and Hosea had all written about a time when these events would take place. They had spoken of the very things that Jesus had just done before their eyes and said clearly that this would be a sign that the Messiah was here. There could be no doubt. John had made no mistake. Jesus was indeed the One who John had said He was.

As the day slowly came to a close, Jesus was eating dinner with a Pharisee when a woman who had lived a very sinful life entered the house uninvited. Pouring an expensive bottle of perfumed oil on His feet and sobbing uncontrollably, she began wiping His feet with her long, dark hair.

Simon, the Pharisee, immediately became annoyed at this display of emotion. If this Jesus was a true prophet, he reasoned to himself, He would know what kind of sinful woman this person was.

Jesus, correcting Simon, pointed out the truth.

In front of all who were there, He reminded Simon that when He entered the house, Simon did not wash His feet, as was the custom for guests. He did not greet Him in the usual way that a guest was to be greeted. He did not anoint His head with oil. But this woman did all these things. She even washed His feet with expensive oil she had purchased with her own money, wiping them dry with her hair. And for all this she expected nothing.

Now, as Simon fumed in anger, Jesus turned back to her and said, "Your sins are forgiven. Your faith has saved you. Go in peace."

Though the dinner at Simon's home was now over, the needs of the people were not, and Jesus, with His disciples in tow, continued on their way. After they had finished in one place, it seemed another would appear before them. There were so many people and so many needs.

As they continued toward the lake, many more people came to see Him. Many had been healed already and simply wanted to thank Him again. Many, too, came with their family and friends whom He had also healed and taught.

Finally they reached the shore, and Jesus and his disciples climbed into a boat. They needed to get across the small lake, known as the Sea of Galilee, and this was the best way to do it.

The disciples, many of whom were fishermen and were used to working with boats, pulled the small craft away from shore and started toward the other side of the lake. Jesus, exhausted from the long day lay down in the boat and soon fell asleep.

The storm clouds formed quickly, rapidly rising and changing into huge boiling thunderheads. Inside the clouds, winds began to rotate and swirl around and around, reaching speeds of well over a hundred miles per hour. The disciples who were fishermen had seen this type of thing before but never a storm this large and happening this quickly.

As the first drops of rain began to hit them, they knew they were in trouble. A swirling hurricane of vicious wind and cold rain seemed to reach down at them, grabbing the water around the small boat that was now struggling to survive. Waves rose above them, crashing down on them time and time again drenching them to the bone, and tossing their boat out of control.

Up, up, over a high wave they were lifted, only to be tossed down again into the sea. There seemed to be no escape from this monster storm. It was only a matter of time. They were going to drown, and they were going to drown soon.

As the panicking men were about to call out to God to help them they suddenly remembered that Jesus was on board with them! They had been so busy trying to save themselves, they had forgotten about Him.

Looking around, they were stunned at what they saw! Jesus was in the stern of the boat, asleep. Asleep? How was that possible?

"Teacher, save us! Don't You care that we are going to die?" they screamed at Him.

Jesus woke up and looked at the terrified men. Then, turning back to the storm He said, "Peace, be still."

Immediately the wind became calm and the waves became still. Looking across at His astonished followers, He simply asked them, "Why are you so fearful? Where is your faith?"

Finally the disciples understood what it was to be absolutely helpless and have no other hope but God. Now they could better understand how the lepers, the paralyzed, and the sick felt. From now on they would have a totally new respect and understanding of how others felt when they had problems no one in the world could solve but God.

But now, a single question began to fill their thoughts. "Who is this, that even the winds and the sea obey Him?"

Rachael had seen the storm, but being an angel, she had also seen what humans could not. This had been no normal storm. This storm had been created by something evil.

Satan was furious that Jesus had calmed his storm. Many times now, he had tried to get rid of Jesus. He had tried to use Herod to kill Him as a baby but had failed. He had tried snakes but had failed. He had tried Pharisees but had failed, and now this. Still, he would not give up. Someday he would get Jesus, and then all of heaven would see who was in charge. They would worship him yet.

26

Life after John

The girl was young, tanned, and beautiful and knew how to dance before a king. She smiled, flashing her eyes at him as she twisted and swirled and danced. And Herod loved every minute of it.

It didn't matter to Herod that she was the daughter of his new wife Herodias, who had been married to his brother Philip until recently. She was young and attractive and it was his birthday. All of his friends were enjoying her too. Maybe they had had too much wine, but no one cared. He was the king and no one told a king what he couldn't do.

As soon as the dance ended, she smiled again at a delirious Herod. With a wave of his hand he called her over to tell her how much he had enjoyed her dance. Not knowing when to stop, he blurted out, "Whatever you ask me, I will give it to you, even up to half of my kingdom."

Thanking him, she returned to her mother to discuss what request to make of the king. "What will I ask for?" the girl wondered aloud. Herod had just offered her half of his kingdom. She could ask for anything. Gold. Jewels. Land. Property. Anything! But her mother had something else on her mind: hatred.

Rotting in a dungeon just a few floors below was the man who had humiliated her in front of everyone, saying that Herod should never have married her. Nobody spoke that way about her. Nobody. She had pushed and nagged Herod until he had finally arrested John, yet still Herod would not agree to kill him.

But her opportunity had finally come. Now she would have her revenge. "Go tell the king that what you want most is to see the head of John the Baptist on a plate," she told her daughter. "That's what we want. That's the only thing we want." The fact that it was only what *she* wanted did not seem to even enter the girl's mind.

Amazingly, she didn't even question her mother's decision. So evil was this family that she was not even surprised or upset about this selfish and hateful request.

Quickly, the request was made and it was made publicly, in front of Herod's friends Though he did not want to have John killed, Herod knew that he had no choice but to grant her request. To back down now would make him look weak in front of everyone, and in King Herod's world, that could never happen. And so he agreed.

Herod had the call sent to the executioner, and within fifteen minutes, the bloody, still-warm head of John the Baptist lay staring up at them from a silver plate.

Rachael had been there, watching during the whole disgusting evening. She had known what was going to happen and had tried to prepare herself, but that didn't mean she had to like it! She didn't. The time would come when all of them would pay for this insane cruelty, but that time was in God's hands, not hers. She trusted God to do what was right.

Now, as John the Baptist was brutally tossed from this world in which he had lived and preached and taught and baptized, Rachael smiled at him as he opened his eyes. Looking up at her, he gasped in surprise and amazement. John the Baptist had just arrived in Paradise.

Meanwhile back on earth, it didn't take long for John's disciples to hear what had happened to their leader. Although they were still mourning the loss of the one they had followed and loved so much, they went to the palace at Machaerus. They did not go to protest. They did not go for revenge. They went there to get the body of their friend and teacher.

The guards at the palace knew immediately who they were. Calling Herod, they asked him what they should do. "Give them their request," Herod ordered. And so the body of John the Baptist was carried away, taken home, and buried in a tomb.

What will He do? His disciples wondered when they told Jesus about John's death. John had been His cousin and friend. He had baptized Him and announced that He was "the Lamb of God that takes away the sins of the world." Maybe Jesus would go and bring John back to life. Maybe He would make fire and brimstone fall down on Herod. *It would serve the butcher right!*

But, after hearing the news, Jesus took all of them with him to a deserted place at the north shore of the Sea of Galilee called Bethsaida. For a while, they just sat and thought about John and the things that had happened while waiting for Jesus to say something. Some of them thought that maybe it was time for Him to take over the world and destroy Rome. If He did, they would be right there with Him.

And then, as they had so many times before, the people came. There were thousands of them who needed to be healed and to be shown love instead of hate. The crowd continued to grow. It seemed as if every person in Galilee came that day to this field on a hill. The numbers were now reaching five thousand men who had not only come themselves, but who had brought their wives and children with them. In all, there were now a total of about fifteen to twenty thousand people sitting on the hill overlooking the Sea of Galilee.

Glancing over at Philip, Jesus asked, "Where do you think we can buy food for all of these people?"

Philip, not really answering the question but observing that they now had a problem, replied, "It would cost a fortune to feed these people even a few bites of bread."

Andrew, who had heard their conversation, suggested a sharing solution might work. "There is a boy here who has five loaves of bread and two small fish." As soon as he said this, he realized how silly it would be to believe they could feed that many people with so little food. So he added, "But what are they among so many?"

"Make the people sit down," Jesus told them. It would take a while for twenty thousand people to get the message. When they were seated, forty thousand eyes stared at Jesus and wondered what He was about to do.

Calling the young boy with the bread and fish to come to Him, Jesus asked him if he was willing to share his lunch with the others. Nodding shyly, the boy handed Jesus his small basket.

Jesus then thanked His Father not only for the boy and his willingness to share but also for what they were about to eat. Handing food to the disciples, they began passing the bread and fish out to the crowd. As they did, an amazing thing happened. The food refused to run out. It seemed that the more food they handed out to people the more food appeared.

Five, ten, fifteen, and then twenty thousand people ate all the bread and fish they wanted. Later, as they gathered up the remaining food, they were stunned to discover how much remained. Twelve baskets full!

The astonished people could only wonder in amazement. *Who is this man?* Nodding in agreement, they concluded that Jesus must truly be the Prophet, written of by Moses, who was to come into the world. They did not realize that this Prophet was the Messiah.

As they began to talk about making Jesus their king, Jesus sent the people home. Then, leaving the city He walked further up the mountain to be alone. He would miss John the Baptist. News of his murder would soon reach Mary, His mother. It would be a hard thing for her to have to hear.

He needed to spend time with His Father. He needed to know what His Father wanted Him to do. He remembered the desert and the lessons He had learned there. He must not allow the world or Satan to push Him in the wrong direction. And so He prayed.

His disciples found Him praying and waited for Him to tell them what He wanted them to do next.

"Go ahead," He suggested. "Take the boat back to Capernaum, and I'll meet you soon."

Getting into the boat, they began their short journey home. Suddenly, the wind began to rise out of nowhere and began to slam against their boat. As the wind increased, it became impossible to row, even for the men who had been fishermen for many years. Finally, about three or four miles from land, they realized that they were making no progress at all in the fierce gale.

Each man remembered the storm that had nearly taken their lives only a short time ago, but this time, Jesus was nowhere to be seen. As the wind howled and the waves rose, they grew more and more afraid. Far from shore and with Jesus still on the hill, they had never felt more alone.

As they struggled to keep the boat from capsizing, they began to make out a faint shape. Someone or something was coming through the roaring waves toward the boat. "A ghost!" they shrieked in fear. Now each one of them thought they would surely die. *If only Jesus had been here He could have saved us*, they thought, as water poured into the boat. The familiar voice shook them back from their panic and terror. "Be of good cheer. It is I; don't be afraid," Jesus called.

Jesus, not a ghost, was walking on top of the sea, approaching them through the wind and spray. As they realized who it was, hope again returned, driving away the terror they had endured only moments ago. They would be OK. Jesus was not going to let them drown. Again, they were going to live.

Peter suddenly stood up in the boat and called out, "Lord, if it's You, command me to come to You on the water."

Though the words seemed silly, Jesus agreed. "Come," He said.

Stepping out of the boat, Peter started out quite well, keeping his eyes on Jesus in front of him. But the task was too great. Looking at the waves and feeling the strength of the wind, he suddenly realized what he was actually doing. Immediately, he began to sink. "Lord, save me!" was all he had time to blurt out as he felt himself slipping down into the water.

Reaching out His hand, Jesus grabbed Peter, pulling him to safety. Softly, He reminded the once confident Peter, "O you of little faith, why did you doubt?"

As Jesus entered the boat, the storm immediately stopped, just as it had the last time. There were no waves. There was no wind. There was no water slamming over the boat. All was calm and still. And then the boat was on the shore.

Satan again foamed with rage. "How many more times will you fail me?" he screamed at the demons he had ordered to get rid of these idiot followers of Jesus. "Get out of my sight now!" he bellowed. Next time, I'll handle things myself."

27

The Lessons of the Storms

Jesus' disciples sat thinking near a campfire. They had seen and experienced so much that their heads were now swimming. They couldn't stop thinking about the two storms that had almost taken their lives. Soon they would come to understand why they had gone through those things, but right now none of it made much sense.

Over and over again these stories would be told, around campfires, during meals, and whenever they met together. They would share the excitement of almost dying at sea and then seeing Jesus calm the wind and waves. "Remember the time when . . . ?" they would ask each other. But the importance of the storms would remain a secret. At least for a while.

Not even Rachael knew the secret of the two storms, and she was wondering about it as Gabriel showed up beside her. "Hi Gabriel. Do you know the meaning of the storms?" she asked. "I know that they must mean something."

"Not entirely," he replied. "There are still a few things that we haven't been able to put together yet. You are right about one thing: everything means something. There is a message in these storms. They are important."

But Jesus knew. While Satan had been attempting to destroy the disciples, Jesus used this time to plant a secret message for every man, woman, and child who would ever place their trust in Him.

The campfire crackled as the disciples talked and ate together. Jesus smiled at His disciples as they relaxed together around the food they were now finishing, remembering the things they had seen and done.

"It's time I explained something to you," He said as the firelight flickered on their faces. "Remember the storms that almost drowned you a few days ago?"

Each man nodded his head. How could they forget?

"These were given to you as lessons," Jesus explained. "You need to understand these lessons and tell them to those who will follow after you in the years to come."

And so He explained how the storms were really a picture of how they should trust Him with their lives. "There will be many storms in your lives," Jesus explained to them. "They may not be wind and waves on the water, but at times you will have problems and struggles that are too hard for you to deal with on your own. When this happens, you need to know that I am able to calm that storm, help you, and bring you peace. When you were in the boat fighting the waves, you forgot that I was in the boat with you. When you realized that you could not save yourself, you called on Me for help. And what happened?"

"You made the storm quiet down," they replied.

"I did. Remember, you are My children. I will help you anytime you need Me. Don't forget to ask Me."

"What about the second storm?" they asked.

"Do you remember where I was when you got into trouble?" Jesus asked them.

"You were still on land. You were on the hill praying," they replied.

"I was," Jesus acknowledged. "This then is the lesson. Right now I am with you, just as I was when I was in the boat. There will come a time, though, when I will not seem to be with you. Someday I will return to My Father and you will not be able to see Me.

"When I was on the hill speaking with My Father, you didn't think I was with you. You thought I was too far away to help! But what happened?"

"You came to us on the water," Peter replied, clearly remembering the whole event.

"You thought I was a ghost or a spirit," Jesus reminded them. "One day when I go to be with My Father in Heaven, I will send you a Comforter, who is the Holy Spirit. He will be your Helper just as I have been. Just because you may not be able to see Me that doesn't mean I have left you alone to face your problems. Remember, no matter what you are going through, I will never ever be too far away to help you. I will never leave you or forsake you."

The disciples nodded, agreeing that they understood what Jesus was saying. The time would soon come when they would need to remember these lessons.

As Jesus continued to preach throughout the land, He reminded the people not to follow Him simply because He had fed them on a hill. Food that we eat and goes into our stomachs does not satisfy us for long. Soon we are hungry again. The words that He was teaching, however, were like food that would last forever. They were wise and good and helpful, especially in times of trouble. "Don't work for food that goes bad," He cautioned. "Work for food that will last forever and the everlasting life which I can give you. I am the bread of life.

Later, Jesus would tell people that He was the water of life. In the same way that water is necessary for life here on earth, so also is it important to know that by trusting Jesus, a person can have eternal life in Heaven. "If anyone thirsts, let him come to Me and drink," He said. Some understood what He was saying. Many did not.

Some of the Temple Guard's officers, who had been listening, reported back to the High Priest the things Jesus was saying and doing. They had heard Jesus claim that he was the bread of life and the water of life. They had seen Him heal the sick. They had noticed that Jesus looked right at them when He said, "Do not make judgments according to what you feel, but judge with honest judgment."

"Why haven't you brought Him in?" shouted the priests.

Shaking their heads, the officers simply replied, "No man ever spoke like this man!"

The priests were disgusted. "So you are deceived too," they snorted. "None of the rulers or Pharisees believe in Him. Only the ignorant crowds swallow this nonsense."

Nicodemus was there, listening and tried to think of what he should say. There was no doubt in his mind that Jesus was the Messiah. He had seen too much to doubt anymore. But no one was listening.

Finally, he decided to remind them of their own laws. "Does our law judge a man before it hears him and knows what he is doing?" he asked.

"Are you from Galilee too?" they said. "Check and see. No prophet has ever come out of Galilee." But even here they were wrong. Jonah and Nahum had both come from this northern region. The priests simply didn't want to hear it. And so they continued trying to come up with a plan to get rid of Jesus forever.

Nicodemus had been giving the situation a lot of thought. He knew about their plans. He knew they were trying to find a way to arrest Jesus and have Him killed. The Pharisees and the scribes hated Him so much that they had lost their ability to know what was true. It was no use even to bring up the subject with them now. It was just as Jesus had been saying. They were blind.

But there was one other possibility that Nicodemus had been thinking about. Though he was one of the most respected scholars and teachers in Israel at that time, another man was also greatly respected. He was a lawyer and a teacher and his name was Gamaliel.

Gamaliel had a brilliant mind and knew the Scriptures as well as anyone, even Nicodemus. He was even training a number of young followers not only to know the law but also to apply it with wisdom and courage.

What if he, Nicodemus, could spend some time with Gamaliel and explain what he knew about Jesus of Nazareth to him? With the support of a teacher like Gamaliel, maybe together they would be able to change the minds of the Pharisees. It would be risky, but he felt it was certainly worth a try.

28

The Rescue

Sarah wondered how her relationship with Nathan had come to this. It was never supposed to be this way. A relationship with a married man who was not her husband. Even after all the things he had told her about what it was like at his home—the loveless marriage, the insults from his wife, the shouting—she still knew it was wrong. She really felt sorry for him, but it was still wrong.

Tonight she was going to end it. Tonight it would be over. As she picked her way down the ancient, dark streets of Jerusalem, Sarah looked over her shoulder into the night. The eerie feeling of being followed bothered her. She could see no one, but still the feeling remained.

She wondered who would be following her. If it was anybody it was probably Nathan's father, Levi. Levi, an important Pharisee, had never believed his son could do anything right on his own. He had forced his son to marry into a wealthy family at a very young age, simply to increase his own family power and importance.

He didn't really care about his own son, his daughter-in-law, or his wife, for that matter. He only truly cared about power. He was cruel and dangerous and Sarah shuddered at the very thought of him. If he ever found out about the relationship between her and Nathan, there would be no limit to what he would do.

There it was again. Footsteps. She turned. No one there. Quietly she turned into a small alley, following it to the next street. She turned left and stopped at a space between two shops. The shops were both closed now, so she nestled in between them and waited, her heart thumping in her chest as she tried to calm down. Maybe she was just imagining things. At least tonight would be the last time she would have to meet Nathan like this—in secret.

She waited between the shops for what seemed like ten minutes. Then she peeked out carefully. Again, nothing.

Normally Jerusalem would be pitch black by now, but tonight there was a full moon that shone over the city, throwing long, dark shadows along the houses, shops, and streets. At least she didn't need a lamp tonight. This would have told anyone following her where she was.

She doubled back and around through the old streets, looking carefully to see if anyone might be following her. It would be far more difficult to keep from being found if anyone was actually on her trail. She couldn't hear any footsteps now. Maybe she had lost them.

Carefully, she walked toward her destination again. She was going to a small house where Nathan would be waiting for her. She was late now. She needed to hurry.

She climbed the steps to the house and tapped softly on the door. It opened almost immediately, startling her, until she realized it was Nathan.

"I felt someone was following me," she whispered, "but I think I lost them."

"That's impossible," he replied. "Who would be following you?" But he knew the answer as soon as he asked the question. "My father has no idea about us!" he thought out loud.

She knew she had to get this conversation over with as soon as possible so she looked at him and blurted it out, "Nathan, there is no more 'us'! I can't do this anymore. You need to fix things with your wife. I have to go now. You're a good man, Nathan. Goodbye."

As Nathan struggled to come up with something to say, she lifted herself up on her tiptoes and kissed him on the cheek. Suddenly, there was a huge bang as the door was smashed open. Before they could react, two men rushed in to grab Nathan, holding him down as he struggled to break free. As they held him, his father entered the room and grabbed Sarah by the arm.

"So, my dear," he sneered, "it looks as if you have been caught in the act of adultery. The penalty for that, by the way, is death."

"Let her go!" shouted Nathan. "She's done nothing wrong. You can see nothing has happened."

Levi looked at him, snorting in disgust. "Keep him here," he barked at the men. Turning to Sarah while continuing to hold her arm, he hissed, "You, come with me."

Levi and another Pharisee dragged Sarah out of the house and down the stairs. At first she struggled to break free, but they were far too strong and she soon gave up.

Dragging her along, they made their way to the Temple. Here, she was thrown into a storage room as if she was a bag of garbage. With that, they slammed the door behind her and locked it. As Sarah lay there in the small, dark room with tears flowing down her cheeks, she felt more alone and terrified than she had ever been in her whole life.

Leaving the Mount of Olives where He had spent the night, Jesus walked down the hill, crossing the Kidron brook on his way up to the Temple. As was the case wherever He went now, it took no time at all for crowds of people to find Him, begging Him to either heal them or to teach them. Today He began to teach.

The noise and shouting grew louder as they approached. It was the Pharisees and the scribes again, and today they had not come to hear Jesus teach. This time they had a brand new problem they wanted Him to deal with. The problem was the young woman they were dragging with them. She was exhausted and scared and crying, but they didn't care. She was simply a piece of bait to them. She was a tool they could finally use to catch Jesus.

Levi had gotten the mob together and the mob wanted blood. The Pharisees roughly tossed Sarah on the ground in front of Jesus. She looked up at Jesus for a moment, then, in embarrassment looked away again. To her, this was just another rabbi who would never believe her or even try to help. She truly believed that she would die that day, and no one would even care.

And so the Pharisees began the test.

Sarah finds herself before Jesus.

"Teacher," Levi lied, "this woman was caught in adultery, in the very act. In the law, Moses said that anyone who does this should be put to death by stoning. But what do You say?"

Jesus listened but said nothing. He chose not to remind this arrogant man that the law he was referring to required both the man and the woman to be brought forward for their sin. But Levi couldn't care less about the young woman's sin. He simply wanted to trap Jesus by getting Him to say something that was wrong.

Gently, Jesus stooped to the ground and began to write something in the sandy clay with His finger.

"What do You say, Teacher?" Levi continued. "Give us an answer."

Rising up, Jesus looked at them. "He who is without sin among you, let him throw the first stone at her," He said. With that, He began writing on the ground again.

When the Pharisees looked down at the sand to see what Jesus was writing, each one of them saw a list of sins that they themselves had committed. And it was a big list.

Shocked, Levi looked down to see things there *he* had done. *How does this man know?* Levi wondered, worried now that Jesus might tell the others what he had done. If Jesus said anything, he would deny it, but he certainly didn't want to take that chance. Some might believe it and his reputation would be ruined. He really didn't want to stick around to see if that would happen.

It seemed to only take a moment. One by one, all the men had slipped away, from the oldest down to the youngest. Amazingly, even Levi snuck away, his plan to trap Jesus now spoiled.

Alone now with Sarah, Jesus stretched Himself up onto His feet again. "Where did all those accusers of yours go?" He asked her. "Isn't anyone left to condemn you?"

Sarah looked around. Not a single person remained. "No one, Lord," was all she could say as her heart still pounded with fear. Then she heard the words that she would remember for the rest of her life.

"Neither do I condemn you; go and sin no more."

As Sarah left the Temple that day, she knew she had been forgiven. She had met the Master. He had not condemned her. He actually cared about her. She had just experienced God's grace. For the first time in her life, she was free.

29

Blindness and Sight

Being blind two thousand years ago was an awful thing to endure. There were no schools for blind people to teach them how to deal with their disability. There were no "Seeing Eye dogs" to help them get around. There was no play, no work, no money and no respect. You were considered to be a disappointment and treated as if you were almost worthless. You begged and took whatever you were given. You lived that way until you died.

Aaron knew exactly how it felt. He knew how it felt because he had been born blind. He had never seen the rich blue color of the sky or the dark green of the sea. He had never seen the sun break through a cloudy day or a sunrise or a sunset. He had never seen a flower in a garden, a tree in a forest, or a grassy meadow sparkling with fresh dew. As a child, he had never played with other children. He had never even had a close friend.

His world was dark, and his life was lonely; but his other senses of hearing, touch, taste and smell were sharp, and his mind was alert and smart. He knew far more about what was going on around him than many who could see clearly. Even though people sometimes treated him as if he wasn't there, he was, and he paid attention. Just like today.

It began as he sat by a wall, feeling the warm sun he had never seen and begging for food. The voices were faint at first, but grew louder as some men approached. "Rabbi, who sinned, this man or his parents, that he was born blind?" a man asked.

He knew they were obviously talking about him as if he couldn't hear them. And what did they mean about him being blind because he had somehow sinned before he was even born? How did that work? How was this Rabbi going to answer that? Aaron wondered.

Indeed, he had spent many years asking himself many of these same questions. Why had he been born blind? Had he sinned in a previous life? He may be blind, but he certainly knew the Scriptures well enough to know that was not possible. Was he being punished because of something his parents had done?

"Go ahead, Rabbi Whatever-Your-Name-Is. Give it your best shot," he muttered under his breath. "Tell them why I'm blind."

The answered came quickly and it came as a complete surprise. "Neither this man nor his parents sinned, but that God's work should be revealed in him," the Rabbi replied. Aaron missed the next words, but he heard what followed. "As long as I am in the world, I am the light of the world."

What did this all mean? Who was this man that spoke with such a gentle, soft voice yet with so much authority?

As Aaron listened, he felt movement. Someone was getting down beside him. Now someone was touching his face and smearing soft mud on his eyes. Then Aaron heard the man with the gentle voice speak to him saying, "Go wash in the pool of Siloam." Aaron tried to find out what was going on, but the Voice and His friends were already gone.

Alone now, and remembering the instructions the Voice had told him, he rose to his feet and stumbled off toward the Siloam pool. He knew that it was in the southeastern corner of the city, so he went.

Though Rachael mostly watched over and protected children, she also frequently kept an eye on those who could not help themselves. Normally, she remained invisible so no one would even know she was there, however today she was keeping an eye on Aaron and had taken on the form of an old and somewhat slow man. This would allow her to stay back with him as he felt his way along without it being too obvious.

Keeping close beside him, she helped prevent him from tripping and falling, sometimes kicking objects that were in his path out of the way. Aaron had no idea this was happening of course and felt he was doing quite well on his own at moving around the people in the crowded streets.

As they reached the pool of Siloam, Rachael eased out of the way as Aaron made his way to the edge of the pool and bent down to wash the mud from his eyes. Rachael always loved this part and watched closely as Aaron was about to receive the surprise of his life. Kneeling at the pool, he began to wash away the mud that Jesus had placed over his blind eyes. As he did, for the first time in his life, he was able to see some light.

It began as a washing away of darkness, much as we sense early in the morning when the sun begins to produce the first hints of daylight. Gradually, as he worked away the mud, the light gently grew and melted into shapes of things he had never seen before. He knew what they were, but he had never seen them until now. Before him was water. It sparkled in the noon sun. It shone back at him through shimmering ripples and flashing movement.

Suddenly he saw something completely unexpected just below the water's surface. A face! He moved. The face moved. He moved again. The face moved again. It was his face. This must be what he looked like. He had never even imagined how others saw him. This was what he looked like.

As he stared and stared at the face in the water, he realized that this was the first gift of true sight; seeing yourself as you really are.

He looked up and saw the sky. He didn't know the name of its color, but it was beautiful beyond words.

These must be people. He stared at them, watching their movements. Fascinated, he watched their feet, arms, hands, and heads, all moving with perfect timing.

Looking to his left, he saw an old man with a wonderfully kind face smiling at him. Aaron smiled back. "I can see!" he shouted. "I can see! Do you understand? I was blind and now I can see!"

The old man continued to smile at him and nodded. Oddly, he didn't seem surprised at all. "To be able to see is a wonderful gift, isn't

Rachael watches as Aaron receives his sight.

it? I am so happy for you. Go in peace, Aaron," he said as he turned and walked slowly away. Still in shock over his first moments of sight, it took a few seconds for Aaron to put things together. As he walked back the way he had come, a question formed in his mind. *How did he know my name?*

Reaching the place where he used to beg, Aaron asked the people there if they remembered the man with the voice who had spoken with him and put mud on his eyes. Many could not, but one did. He told Aaron that the man's name was Jesus.

It didn't take long for people to find out that Aaron the beggar could now see! People knew him as the blind beggar and where he lived. They knew he had always been blind, and now he could see! The question was, how?

"What happened?" they asked. Every time, Aaron would tell them the same thing. "A man called Jesus put mud on my eyes and told me to wash in the pool of Siloam. I did, and now I can see."

Because of all that had happened and with his neighbors' urging him, Aaron went with them to the Temple to thank God for his sight. There he first ran into the Pharisees, and they did not take the news well at all.

"Who did this?" the one named Levi asked.

"A man called Jesus," Aaron answered.

"And when did this happen?"

"Today."

"Today?"

"Yes, today."

The Pharisees looked at each other in surprise and anger. This Jesus was doing it again, healing people on the Sabbath, right under their very noses. Now the Pharisees questioned whether it was legal to heal on the Sabbath. Levi said, "Absolutely not!" On the other hand, some said, "Maybe it is! How could Jesus do such things if He was not from God?"

Turning to Aaron, they asked, "So, what do you say?"

For the first time Aaron had a chance to say what he felt. "He is a prophet," he stated simply.

Not convinced, the Pharisees now announced that Aaron had never been blind in the first place. There, that solved the problem! No miracle, no laws broken! All we have here is a lying beggar who is looking to make trouble. Case solved.

But it was not that simple. Aaron had parents. One quick conversation with them confirmed the Pharisees' worst nightmare. Aaron had been healed.

Basically, the conversation went this way: "Yes, this is our son. No, we don't know what happened. Yes, he was born blind and can now see clearly. If you want to know what happened, ask him."

Oops. The problem was back. It was now time to talk to Aaron again. "Listen," Levi began. "We know this man is a sinner. Why don't you just admit that God healed you and leave Jesus out of it."

Aaron was almost starting to enjoy this. "Well, I don't know anything about whether or not He is a sinner, but I do know this: once I was blind, but now I see."

So, on and on they argued about who Jesus was. Finally in frustration, they blurted out, "You are His disciple but we are Moses' disciples. We know that God spoke to Moses, but as for this guy, we have no idea where He is from."

Aaron had now had enough. He couldn't help himself. "Well, isn't this a marvelous thing," he began. "He opened my eyes, and you can't figure out where He's from. We know God doesn't hear sinners, only those who worship Him. Just name one time in history when anyone opened the eyes of a blind man. If this man were not from God He could do nothing."

The Pharisees had also had enough. Their thinking was, if you can't reason with someone just insult him. "Well, you're just an ignorant sinner too!" they shouted as they pushed him out of the Temple.

Not far from the pool of Siloam, Aaron heard a familiar voice. Turning around, for the first time, he looked into the face of the One who had given him his sight. "Jesus!" he exclaimed.

"Do you believe in the Son of Man?" Jesus asked him, using another term that was understood to mean the Messiah.

"Who is He, Lord?" Aaron asked.

Then, so there could be no doubt, Jesus told him, "You are looking at Him and speaking to Him right now."

Aaron knew it was true. It didn't matter what anybody else said. Jesus had given him the greatest gift of his life and now he could see clearly. "Lord, I believe," he answered, and then he worshiped Him.

Rachael watched quietly, and this time, invisibly. She loved this part too.

30

Life and Death

Though most of Jesus' life was spent in Galilee, several times a year He would make the return trip up to Jerusalem. His journeys to the Holy City were not always to go to the Temple or to drive the Pharisees crazy. Over the last few years, He had become friends with many people in Jerusalem and the surrounding towns. On these trips, Jesus would be able to see them and spend time with them again.

Nicodemus, of course, lived in Jerusalem and so they tried to meet together whenever Jesus was in the area. Because Nicodemus was a Pharisee, they met secretly, away from the prying eyes of the scribes and priests. Nicodemus loved having Jesus in his home. He introduced Jesus to his family, and together they would sit and talk for hours. God the Teacher was now teaching the Teacher of Israel.

Samuel, Rebecca, and Miriam still lived in Bethlehem. Since Jesus had healed Miriam, the news had quickly spread and many people now believed in Him because of what He had done for her. Jesus loved being back in the town of His birth and when Samuel and Rebecca begged Him to stay with them, He agreed. Miriam immediately ran off to find her friends and to bring them back to meet the Teacher who had healed her face and arm.

That evening their home was filled with joy and laughter as they told what had been happening in their lives. Miriam, still amazed and thankful that she had been healed, continued to ask Jesus question after question. He never grew tired of answering them and together they talked on into the night. As they talked, their friendship grew even closer.

About four miles up the road, in another town called Bethany, a man named Lazarus lived with his two sisters, Mary and Martha. They knew everybody and were good friends with Samuel and Rebecca. Like Nicodemus, Lazarus often bought sheep from Samuel. On the day that Miriam had returned to Bethlehem after being healed, Lazarus, Mary, and Martha had danced for joy with Samuel and Rebecca over this great news.

After having spent time with Nicodemus and Samuel, Jesus walked up the road to spend a few days with Lazarus and his family. Their friendship too had become warm and close, after having met only a few months earlier. Finally, after a lengthy visit, it was time for Jesus to leave.

Leaving Lazarus' home, He turned north. His thoughts now turned to how He had come to earth to heal the sick and had accomplished this. He had come to challenge the religious leaders and had done this too. He had also come to open the eyes of those who were willing to see who He really was.

It was time for Him to teach again. God had come to earth to spend time with people, and He wanted them to see what He was really like. And what is God like? To understand this, Jesus said they had to think like a sheep. God was their good shepherd, and Jesus was the God they could see here on earth. He loved His sheep and would do anything for them.

"I am the good shepherd," Jesus said. "I will even lay down My life for My sheep. Not only that, but I will take it up again. As a matter of fact, no one can even take My life from Me. I lay it down Myself."

As the next few days passed, Jesus continued to teach in that area. Some believed Him and saw that He was telling the truth. Others, especially the scribes and priests, did not and continued to look for a chance to kill Him before He became even more popular with the people. That is when the news arrived about Lazarus. He had suddenly become seriously ill.

Mary and Martha were terrified for their brother and sent an urgent message to Jesus, asking him to come. They knew He loved

Lazarus and could heal him. He just needed to get to Bethany quickly before it would be too late.

As Jesus' disciples got ready for the trip back to Bethany, Jesus listened to His Father and remembered the lessons He had learned in the desert, long ago. "This sickness is not unto death," He said, "but for the glory of God, that the Son of God may be glorified through it."

Then, surprisingly, as His disciples wondered why He would not rush to Bethany to heal His friend, Jesus decided to stay where he was for two more days.

After the two days had passed, Jesus finally announced to the disciples that it was time to go to Bethany. Remembering that Judea, where Bethany was, was where the angry Pharisees had almost stoned them to death, the disciples let Jesus know how worried they were. This was dangerous, they thought, and here He was, heading back into trouble again. And He was bringing them with Him.

"Our friend Lazarus sleeps. I need to go back to wake him up," He explained.

Sleeping is good, the disciples thought. If he is able to sleep, that's a sign he's getting better.

Finally, knowing that they were not understanding what He was saying, Jesus said clearly, "Lazarus is dead."

And so, though the disciples were afraid that they might very well be killed by the hate-filled Pharisees, they left with Jesus for Bethany. Because the walk back to Bethany was long and exhausting, it was not surprising that Jesus and His disciples stopped near Jerusalem to rest. Here they planned to spend the night and move on the next morning. As they rested, the news about them traveled quickly even reaching Mary and Martha. "The Master is on His way," they were told.

The next day, as Jesus and His disciples approached the home in Bethany, Martha quickly left, making her way to meet them while Mary, still struggling with the death of her brother, remained in the house.

Approaching her Friend, Martha greeted Jesus sadly. "Lord, if you had been here, my brother would not have died." Then, collecting her thoughts, she added, "But even now I know that whatever You ask of God, He will give You."

Looking straight into her eyes, Jesus replied, "Your brother will rise again."

"I know he will at the resurrection on the last day," she said through her sadness and pain. Yet, the day when all believers would be raised from the dead just seemed so far away. She missed her brother now.

But that is not what Jesus meant. Wanting her to trust Him, even though things looked so hopeless, Jesus pointed to Himself as He said, "I am the resurrection and the life. He who believes in Me, even though he may die, he shall live. Whoever lives and believes in Me, shall never die. Do you believe this?"

Martha felt confused but knew also that if Jesus was asking her if she believed He was telling her the truth, there was only one answer. "I believe You are the Christ, the Son of God," she replied. Turning, she now headed back to the house to tell her sister what had happened. She had to get things ready for Him and tell Mary that Jesus wanted to see her.

As soon as Martha told Mary that Jesus wanted to see her, Mary too left the house to meet Him.

As soon as she saw Jesus, Mary said the same thing that her sister had said. "Lord, if You had been here, my brother would not have died," she blurted out through tears that were now pouring down her cheeks.

"Where is his body?" Jesus asked.

"Come and see," Mary replied, beckoning for Him to follow as others now began joining them.

Surrounded by so much pain and sadness, Jesus too felt Himself being overcome by grief, weeping tears of His own as He made His way to Lazarus' tomb.

Now, with everyone at the tomb, Jesus stared at the sealed door. "Take away the stone," He ordered,

"But Lord, he's been dead for four days now! The smell is going to be really bad," Martha protested.

"Didn't I ask you to believe?" Jesus encouraged her.

So they rolled the stone away from the doorway. Looking around again at the pain and sadness and despair in this place of death, Jesus again spoke to His Father. Thanking Him for always listening to Him and hearing His prayers, He finally turned to the open tomb and shouted, "Lazarus, come out!"

Silence. The people gathered there held their breath, afraid to make a sound. *Surely the dead couldn't come back to life after four days! Yet look at all the things that He's done before.*

Still silence. They waited. No earthquake. No thunder. No voice from heaven.

And then it happened. A man wrapped in strips of cloth (like a mummy) could be seen shuffling his way out of the tomb! Lazarus was alive! Tears of pain turned to tears of joy as everyone realized what was happening. Lazarus was really alive! All around the tomb, people dropped to their knees, shocked at what they were seeing with their own eyes.

"Unwrap the strips of cloth and let him go," Jesus commanded. As the cloth surrounding his face and body was removed, the familiar face of their friend and brother could now be seen, smiling and grinning back at them through the sticky, gluey spices that had held the strips in place.

After a single command from Jesus, their brother and friend, Lazarus, was back with them again, alive and well.

31

The Last Supper

Nicodemus had just returned home from his first meeting with Gamaliel. The previous day, he had pulled the teacher aside while they were in the Temple and told him that he needed to speak with him privately. Because of the growing hatred of Jesus by the High Priest and his Pharisees in Jerusalem, the sooner they met the better.

Gamaliel had eagerly agreed to speak with him, so they met in a secret place where they could discuss Jesus without Levi and the other Pharisees trying to shout them down. Nicodemus decided to trust Gamaliel and tell him all he knew. This was the most dangerous part. If Gamaliel turned against him and told the others, Nicodemus knew he would lose more than his job and position. He would probably lose his life.

As it turned out, Gamaliel was a man of honor. He confessed that he too was upset with the way that Caiaphas (the high priest), Levi, and the others were behaving toward Jesus.

As Nicodemus told story after story about Jesus and the things He had done, Gamaliel could hardly believe his ears. Then, when Nicodemus told him how Miriam had been healed, Gamaliel simply shook his head in amazement.

Together, they both agreed to search the Scriptures to find out more about the Messiah, but as they parted, Nicodemus turned to Gamaliel with one more piece of information: "By the way," he said, "I know someone who will confirm that Jesus of Nazareth was actually born in Bethlehem. As you know, this is the exact place where the prophets said the Messiah would be born."

It did not take long for news of Lazarus to reach the ears of the Pharisees, and almost immediately an emergency council was called to discuss the "problem." They had always hated Jesus and felt He was a trouble-making sinner, but now things were worse. If He was raising the dead, the people would believe in Him and reject them. If that happened, the Roman rulers would take away the Pharisees' position, money, and power. They could not allow that. They were not interested in searching the Scriptures for truth about what Jesus was saying or who He was. This was about holding on to power.

There could be no more waiting. Jesus would need to be put to death, and it would have to be soon.

Jesus knew exactly what the Pharisees were planning to do. He had known all along that this time would come, so now He left with His disciples to a place where they could be together for a few days. There were still things He needed to teach them, and He knew time was running out.

With the Passover only six days away, Jesus and His disciples now returned to Bethany to spend some time with Lazarus, Mary, and Martha. Here, just as the woman in Galilee had done many days before, Mary took a whole bottle of her most expensive perfumed oil. Opening it and pouring it over Jesus' feet, she wiped His feet with her long hair, filling the room with the wonderful fragrance of the scented oil.

Judas, one of the disciples, was disgusted that the oil had been wasted this way. He felt the money should have been given to help the poor, but Jesus corrected him. "Leave her alone," He said. "She is doing this for My burial. You will always have the poor with you, but you will not always have Me."

Finally the time had come for Jesus to leave for Jerusalem where He would celebrate Passover one last time with His disciples. Riding on a young donkey, He approached the city from Bethany. From everywhere, people crowded around Him on the way. Many had seen Him raise Lazarus from the dead, and now they wanted Him to be their king. Cutting palm branches from trees, they waved them before

Him as He made His way past the Mount of Olives and down the hill toward the Kidron brook. "Hosanna!" they cried out, which means "save now." "Blessed is He who comes in the name of the Lord! The King of Israel!"

Though few that day would notice it, another Scripture had just been fulfilled. Five hundred years before this, the prophet Zechariah had said that Israel's king would one day come to them riding on a donkey's colt. The message had come from a time long ago when a king would ride a horse into war. The donkey was a symbol that the king had come in peace.

Watching from a distance, Levi seethed in anger. "Look, the whole world has gone after Him," he muttered to the other Pharisees with him. Then, with a snort, he turned to go. He had a meeting to get to and a murder to plan.

Rachael had seen good times and bad times. She had praised God in the Great Palace and before shepherds. She had helped and cared for Jesus in the desert. She had watched as Jesus had given sight to the blind and healthy legs to people who couldn't walk. But she had also seen what evil men could do, especially when Satan stepped in to cause trouble. She had seen him fall from Heaven and now she saw him take control of Judas Iscariot, one of Jesus' disciples, to have him turn Jesus over to the Pharisees.

She shuddered as she realized what was about to unfold. Jesus had told her in the Great Palace that this would lead to good for the whole world, but before the light could come, it would become very dark indeed.

Levi was happier than he had been in years. Here was this man named Judas, one of Jesus' own disciples, who was offering to turn Him over to them for the unbelievably small sum of thirty pieces of silver. *The fool*, Levi thought. They would have paid ten times that price for Him.

And so it was agreed. Judas would let them know the exact place Jesus and the disciples would be, and he would kiss Jesus on the cheek as a sign that He was the one they should take! Arrangements were made with Caiaphas; a plan was now in place. The Temple guard would be ready and waiting to finally make the arrest. Everything was perfect.

An upper room had been prepared for them and now they were finally gathered together for the last supper they would ever share in this world. The room itself sat high over the place where the Valley Gate had once been, looking out across the Valley of Hinnom. This was where all the garbage of Jerusalem was dumped and burned. A thin layer of smoke caused by the burning garbage acted as a constant reminder that people have garbage in their lives that needs to be removed and destroyed. Though no one knew it yet, there could not have been a more perfect place for a moment such as this. In a few short hours, Jesus of Nazareth would pay for the removal of all the sins and filth, not only of Jerusalem, but also of the entire world.

As they all sat down together to eat, Jesus shared with them how much He had been looking forward to eating this meal with them. He then added, "I say to you, I will not eat a Passover meal again until it is fulfilled in the kingdom of God." Though the disciples would remember these words later, at the time they had no idea He was telling them that this would be their last meal together.

Before they began to eat, Jesus stood up, removed His outer robe, took a bowl of water, and began washing the feet of the men. Everyone knew a mistake had been made. Normally a servant would do this job, but no one had hired a servant, and certainly no one wanted to have to act like one. They were too busy dreaming of how important they would be in Jesus' kingdom. To see Jesus washing their feet was embarrassing, and shame flooded in over their pride.

Peter's protest was immediate, almost ordering Jesus not to do this, but Jesus gently reminded him that if he wanted to be His disciple, he would need to be willing to allow this. And so the washing continued until all the disciples' feet were clean. All, that is, but one. Even though He had just washed Judas' feet, knowing what Judas was about to do, Jesus now looked up at him and said sadly, "You are not all clean."

As the meal began, Jesus had another announcement to make, "One of you will turn against Me," He said, with sadness and compassion in His voice. Immediately everyone began talking at the same time, wondering if Jesus meant him. Quietly, Jesus turned to Judas. "What you do, do quickly," He said simply. With that, Judas left the room, leaving the other disciples to think he was going on an errand. In a way, he was.

With Judas now gone, Jesus picked up a loaf of bread. Breaking it in pieces and passing a piece to each person there, He explained to them that this was now a picture of His body which was about to be broken for them.

Reaching out again, Jesus picked up a cup of wine. He reminded them that the wine would now stand for the blood which He soon would shed for them all. It would become a picture of the new life they were about to receive.

As the meal, which was a reminder of that first Passover so many years ago, continued, they drank the wine, ate the bitter herbs, and enjoyed the roast lamb that had been prepared. Together, they sang the Hallel. These words can be found in Psalm 113 and 114 and were always sung on the eve of Passover.

Both during and after the meal, Jesus continued to tell His disciples many things. He told them to love one another as He had loved them. This was how people would know they were His disciples after He was gone. He told them that He was the way, the truth, and the life, and that no one could come to the Father except through Him. He reminded them that though they had always considered Israel to be the vine, He was the true vine. Just as fruit, like grapes, could only grow if they were attached to the vine, so His followers would only be able live the fruitful lives they should as they themselves remained close and faithful to Him. But difficult times were coming. Not everybody would believe them or treat them well. However, he would be preparing a place for them in Heaven, and one day He would come again so that they would be together with Him forever.

He prayed for Himself because He knew He was soon to face the most difficult time of His life. He prayed for His disciples to be faithful and strong. And he prayed for those of us who would be born on earth in the years to come. Yes, He prayed for you and me. He prayed that we would come to a place in our lives where we would love and trust Him just as these men had done. And then it was time to go.

32

Gethsemane

Leaving the upper room, they made their way down the stairs to the road outside the door. Peter, still upset that anyone would even think of turning against their Master, insisted that he would never think of doing such a thing! But Jesus, knowing what was coming had a word of caution for Peter. That that same night, before the rooster crowed, Peter would not once but three times deny that he even knew Him.

Turning downhill, they walked along the old city wall, past the Temple, and into the Kidron Valley. Crossing the small Kidron brook they climbed the hill known as the Mount of Olives and entered the small garden they had visited so many times before.

It was known as the Garden of Gethsemane, which meant "the olive press." That night, just as the press would squeeze the olive until it burst, Jesus was about to go through the most intense pressing, or pressure, of His life. It was here that Jesus would make the final decision to either allow others to kill Him or to go free.

From His time in the desert until now, Jesus knew that these kinds of decisions should not be made without prayer. Though He had already spoken to His Father in the upper room, He needed to pray again as the time for His arrest quickly approached.

Leaving the others, He brought Peter, James, and John with Him to a private place in the garden. Knowing what He was about to endure, He said to them, "You have no idea how heavy this load is for Me now! It's as if it's crushing the life out of Me and I'm dying! Just stay and watch with Me awhile."

As the sorrow and pressure built up inside of Him, they heard Him cry out, "O My Father, if it is possible, let this cup pass from Me; nevertheless, not as I will, but as You will."

The pressure continued to increase. It was as if God was not listening. Now, turning to His disciples again, He saw they had fallen asleep. "What? Can't you watch with Me an hour?" Then, knowing the things Peter was about to face, He said to him, "Pray that you will not enter temptation!"

But still the pressure continued to increase more and more.

Invisible to the human eye, ten thousand angels watched the drama unfold before them as they stared in horror at the Son of God, now lying on His face in agony, pleading for help.

As Jesus fought His feelings of terror and pain, all Heaven watched what was happening before them. By now they all knew that this was the real reason Jesus had come to earth. This was the test that must be passed. The fate of every person that had ever lived and would ever live hung in the balance. There was no plan "B." This would be successful, or the entire world would fall under Satan's power forever.

Jesus was now in so much pain that even His sweat came out of His skin as huge drops of blood pouring to the ground. As Rachael watched, Gabriel quietly stepped forward and touched Him, laying his hands on Jesus' head and holding them there, waiting. Slowly, Jesus relaxed a little bit, His torment easing off slightly and His strength to handle what lay ahead coming back just enough.

Exhausted, Jesus finally whispered, "Father, if this cup cannot pass away from Me unless I drink it, Your will be done."

It was late when He finally returned to His disciples who had fallen asleep again. Softly, He murmured, "Are you still sleeping? It's time now. I'm being betrayed and handed over to sinful men. Rise up now. Let's be going." Then as He looked up, He said sadly, "See, My betrayer is at hand."

When six hundred soldiers arrive to arrest someone, they aren't usually quiet about it! Tonight was no exception. As soldiers, armed with swords and torches, burst into the garden, Judas led them straight up to where Jesus was standing and greeted Him as if everything was fine. Then, in the greatest act of betrayal in human history, Judas kissed Jesus on the cheek.

"Who are you here to arrest?" Jesus asked, already knowing the answer but wanting to make sure the disciples were not on the soldiers' list as well.

"Jesus of Nazareth!" came the sharp reply.

"I am He," Jesus responded.

Shocked at Jesus' willingness to give Himself up, the soldiers shrunk back in fear. So Jesus asked again, "Who are you seeking?"

Again they said, "Jesus of Nazareth!"

"I have told you I am He. Therefore let these others go their way," Jesus answered.

By now, Peter had had enough, and in an act that could only be called unthinking, he pulled out his sword and swung it at the closest person there! That person was a man called Malchus, the High Priest's servant, who screamed in pain as the sword sliced completely through his right ear, severing it from his head.

Turning to Peter, Jesus instructed him, "Put away the sword, for those who take up the sword will die by the sword. Don't you think that I could ask My Father and He would give Me seventy thousand angels?"

Unseen by human eyes, Rachael watched and waited as over seventy thousand angels stood ready to act the moment they were given the order to help. But the moment never came. Instead of calling for the help He knew was there, Jesus simply reached out and healed Malchus' ear completely.

Having no choice but to follow orders, the captain and his soldiers now tied Jesus' hands, forcing Him to go with them to the house of Annas, the father-in-law of Caiaphas, the high priest. Now the questioning would begin, and it would last all night.

33

The Long Night

The messenger at the door did not bring good news to Nicodemus. Jesus of Nazareth had been arrested and because he was a member of the Sanhedrin, or Supreme Court, Nicodemus had to attend the trial. And they wanted him there now.

"But it's illegal to have a trial at this hour!" Nicodemus objected.

"I don't know about that. But Caiaphas wants you to come right away," the messenger replied simply. "I wouldn't make him wait if I were you."

"Well, you're not me," Nicodemus muttered under his breath. But he knew the young man was right. If Jesus was going to be on trial, he didn't want to make things worse for Him by upsetting Caiaphas now. Better get going, he thought, and see what he could do to help.

When he arrived at the trial, he realized the situation was really bad. Earlier, he and Gamaliel had run out of time as they had tried to talk some sense into the rest of the Pharisees, who now hated Jesus so much they were willing to break all the rules just to get rid of Him. And Nicodemus had a sick feeling that there was nothing he could do to stop them.

Annas was delighted at how everything had turned out. Here before him was this Man who had been causing so much trouble, and he could hardly wait to start grilling Him. "So, tell me about what You believe, and who Your disciples are," he demanded. This too was an illegal question. No one could force another person to give testimony against himself. Any charges should have been brought against Jesus before an arrest had ever been made.

"I have always taught in the open, in synagogues, and in the Temple and have never kept what I believe a secret. Why are you asking Me this? Ask the people I taught," Jesus responded.

Smack! "Don't answer the High Priest like that!' shouted an officer as he struck Jesus across the face.

"If I have spoken evil, say so, otherwise why do you strike Me?" He asked easily.

Now Jesus was quickly moved to Caiaphas' palace where the high priest began throwing more questions at Him. With the Sanhedrin now assembled there, false witnesses, who had been quickly brought in and paid to say what the priests wanted, began to lie about what they had heard Jesus say. Most of the questions seemed to be centered around Jesus saying that he would rebuild the Temple in three days, but they could not even agree about the words they had heard Him say.

Frustrated, Caiaphas finally asked, "Are you the Christ?"

Jesus' response was clear and direct. "I am," He said, "and you will one day see the Son of Man sitting at the right hand of Power, and coming on the clouds of heaven."

Jesus had just said that not only was He the Messiah, but that one day He would judge Caiaphas when He came again. With this, Caiaphas immediately flew into an uncontrollable rage. Tearing his clothes and turning to the Sanhedrin around him, he screamed, "Blasphemy! He has spoken blasphemy! What need do we have of witnesses anymore? What do you say?"

Nicodemus knew he couldn't stop what was going to happen. Along with a friend of his, a Saducee named Joseph of Arimathea, he would not vote against the One he knew was the Messiah. Both men refused to say that Jesus was a liar worthy of death.

But it was no use. "He deserves to die," the Sanhedrin answered as they began spitting on Jesus and beating Him with their hands.

Meanwhile, Peter was having trouble of his own as he waited and warmed himself by a fire outside of the room where the trial was taking place. "You're one of His disciples, aren't you?" a servant girl asked.

Suddenly, Peter, who had shown so much courage in the garden, felt a flood of fear wash over him. "I am not!" he replied sternly.

"You are one of His disciples," another servant said.

"I am not," Peter replied again.

"But I saw you there," he insisted.

"Look, I wasn't there, and I don't know what you're talking about," Peter replied again, this time cursing to make his lie seem more believable. And then, just as Jesus had told him earlier, a rooster crowed.

Remembering what Jesus had said, Peter suddenly realized what he had done. He had just told these people that he didn't even know the very Friend he had promised never to betray! How could he have been so weak? Placing his hands over his face in shame, he began to sob and weep uncontrollably.

Back at the trial, Nicodemus had seen enough. This was the most unbelievable display of cruelty and disregard for the law that he had ever seen in his life, and he had seen a lot. The trial had been at night. The judges had already made up their minds about Jesus being guilty. Someone had paid the witnesses to lie. No one was allowed to defend Jesus. And now, there they were, striking and spitting on the Messiah.

Why was Jesus allowing them to do this? Nicodemus wondered. Surely He would be able to ask God to rescue Him from all of this. So why wouldn't He do this?

Unable to help, Niccodemus knew one thing: he could not be part of this any longer. So, when no one was watching, he left.

With His arms now bound and tied, Jesus was finally led by the soldiers to the dungeon in Caiaphas' palace where He would spend the rest of the night being insulted and beaten by thugs.

After the long night, morning finally broke, and a weary and beaten Jesus was led back to the Sanhedrin again. Picking up the questioning from where it had ended the night before, they began asking Jesus the same questions Caiaphas had asked. Jesus, as He had the night before, gave them the same answers. He told them the truth.

Finally, with no evidence pointing to His guilt, the Sanhedrin pronounced Jesus guilty and deserving of death. Now they needed to drag Him to the governor, Pontius Pilate.

Pilate was still eating breakfast when a servant told him that the chief priests were outside waiting to talk to him. Getting to his feet and making his way to where they had assembled, he saw immediately that they had brought a prisoner to him. "What are the charges against this man?" Pilate asked them.

"If He wasn't an evil-doer, we wouldn't have brought Him to you," they responded with a touch of sarcasm and self-importance.

"OK, go away then and judge Him yourselves," Pilate snapped back. He could play these games too, he thought.

"We would, but we aren't permitted to put anyone to death," they replied, hating the fact that Rome had placed these rules on them in their own country. *Exactly*, Pilate thought. *I'm a Roman, and you need me to do your work for you.*

Turning and leaving the mob of priests, Pilate entered the room where prisoners were interviewed and called for Jesus to be brought to him. "So, are You the King of the Jews?" he asked.

"Are you asking, or are the others?" Jesus answered.

"Am I a Jew?" Pilate snorted in disgust. He hated the Jews, their silly laws, and their whole miserable land. "What have You done?" Pilate finally asked Him.

Jesus agreed to answer his questions. "My kingdom is not of this world. If it was, My servants would fight for My freedom."

"You are a king then," Pilate noted.

"You say I am and you're correct. For this cause I came into the world that I would bear witness to the truth," Jesus answered.

"What is truth?" Pilate muttered as he rose and left the room.

In front of the Jewish leaders, he announced his verdict to them. "I find no fault in Him at all."

But Levi and the other Pharisees would not give up that easily. "Look, He's constantly stirring up trouble throughout all of Judea and even in Galilee," they complained.

Hearing this, Pilate realized that he had an opportunity. He and Herod had been quarrelling lately and this might be a way to fix the hard feelings. Herod had been interested in Jesus for some time now, especially since the murder of John the Baptist, and this would be a great time for Pilate to give him what he wanted: an interview with Jesus of Nazareth.

So Pilate decided to transfer Jesus to Herod's palace so that he could question the man. Things did not go as he planned, however. Herod was delighted to now have the opportunity to interview Jesus, but Jesus refused to talk to Herod. Deciding to have a little fun, Herod had a beautiful purple robe placed on Jesus, then, together with his men, they mocked and bullied Him until they finally became tired of it. Then Herod sent Him back to Pilate.

Now, with Jesus back in his interview room again, Pilate had another idea. Why not make a switch? Heading out to deal with Levi and his priests again, Pilate proposed a solution. "Look," he said, "you have a custom where I release one person of your choosing from my prison at Passover. Do you want me to release your King here, or the criminal Barabbas, who is a thief and robber?"

"Give us Barabbas!" Levi and the Pharisees shouted. "Give us Barabbas!"

Now Pilate was getting worried. His wife had told him not to have anything to do with Jesus because He was innocent and had done nothing wrong. Earlier, she had been shown this in a dream and believed it was true.

Over and over, Pilate had tried his best to convince the chief priests and rulers that Jesus did not deserve death; yet no matter how hard he tried, they still refused to listen.

Back in the room again, Pilate continued asking Jesus question after question but could find nothing at all that he had ever done wrong. He knew exactly why Jesus was here; the Jewish leaders were jealous of Him and they didn't want the people following Him and turning away from them. This whole trial was a fake, and he knew it.

Hoping to ease the hatred that was now becoming more and more intense, Pilate now decided to give the mob some of what they wanted. He had Jesus whipped.

Stripping off the purple robe Jesus had been wearing, the soldiers now tied Him to a stake and whipped Him brutally for crimes that everyone knew He had never committed. With the whipping finished, they placed the robe on him again, and a thorny branch was twisted into a crown of thorns and placed on Jesus' head. Now, barely able to stand, the soldiers again pushed Jesus out in front of the angry mob.

"Behold, your King," Pilate announced to them, hoping for a change of attitude as they looked at what had just been done.

Still, as they looked at Jesus, His face torn and mangled and His body slashed and bloody with the deep, red scars from the whip, they still were not satisfied.

"So now what do you want me to do with Him?" Pilate asked again.

"Crucify Him!" shouted Levi as he encouraged the crowd to say the same thing.

"I find no fault in Him and neither does Herod," Pilate pleaded with the crowd.

"Crucify Him!" they shouted. "Crucify Him!"

"Do you really want me to crucify your King?" he asked, amazed.

"We have no king but Caesar!" Levi shouted back.

Pilate finally gave up. Though he knew what Levi and the crowd were doing and that they only wanted to crucify Jesus so that their own positions of power would be protected, he still didn't want to risk a riot or uprising. Taking a bowl of water and washing his hands in front of the crowd, he looked at them all with disgust. "I am innocent of the blood of this man," he insisted.

Now, even though he had not been able to find a single thing that would make Jesus guilty of death, Pilate handed Jesus over to the mob. "Go ahead, you kill this man yourselves," he told them as he turned and disappeared inside.

With that, the soldiers dragged Jesus away to a place called Golgotha to be crucified.

Only a short distance away, the crowd watched as a dirty, rough, and fearsome looking man made his way out of the prison doors. On his face, a look of puzzled surprise and relief could be seen by any who chose to look.

Barabbas had just been released.

34

Golgotha

Behind the veil where humans cannot see, Rachael waited with over seventy thousand angels, watching as the events before them unfolded. They had waited in the garden, but no order to help Jesus had come. They had watched as Satan seemingly controlled every hateful word and action, yet no order had come. They had watched evil men unfairly accuse, beat, and whip the Jesus they had known and loved since creation, yet no order had come. It seemed so unfair. As tears filled the eyes of these servants of the Living God, they knew what Satan and his evil forces did not: No matter how bad things look, God is still in control. It was not over yet. So they stood guard, and Rachael, holding her breath, waited for what would come next.

Simon of Cyrene was just leaving Jerusalem following Passover. It had been a long trip, and he was now glad to finally be heading home. *Just the sight of the Temple is breathtaking,* he thought, as he stopped to rest for a moment to take it all in. One day soon, he would bring his sons Alexander and Rufus to this place. He could only imagine how excited they would be to see all of this.

The sound of loud talking, shouting, and noise pulled his thoughts away from his family and caused him to turn and look to see what was happening. Soldiers again. They were all over the place today. *Maybe it's because of Passover*, he thought.

As the noise grew louder, he noticed a group of people heading his way. He could see them clearly now. Soldiers, prodding and pushing three men dragging crosses. One in particular was in extremely bad shape. He had been whipped, and even pieces of His beard had been pulled from His face.

As they drew closer, the whipped man stumbled and fell under the weight of His cross. Suddenly a soldier pointed at Simon. "Hey, you. Come over here," he ordered. "Pick up this cross and come with us."

A wave of fear suddenly flooded over Simon, but he moved quickly to obey. If they thought he wasn't going to cooperate with them they might very well do the same to him. Suddenly he was in the middle of all this.

Moving quickly to pick up the cross, Simon, for a brief moment, looked into the man's eyes. Even though the man was suffering, He looked at Simon with compassion and love. As if He knew what Simon was afraid of, the man whispered quietly, "It's OK. This cross is meant for me, not you. Just carry it for me. I'm too weak."

Lifting the cross to his shoulder, Simon took one more look back at the man, "Thank you," He said softly.

Carrying that horrible, wooden cross, Simon wondered the same question so many people had asked before. *Who was this man?* Maybe if he paid attention, he would find out.

Nicodemus had had a long night, tossing and turning after returning home from Caiaphas' palace and still trying to make sense of it all. What he could have done differently? He wondered. How could he have stopped this?

And then, like a bolt of lightning, a memory struck him. That first night he talked with Jesus. What had Jesus said? "As Moses lifted up the serpent in the wilderness, even so must the Son of Man be lifted up, that whosoever believes in Him should not perish but have eternal life."

Nicodemus was stunned. Jesus had known all along. He had been talking about this very moment, the moment He would be crucified. It all made sense now. That's why He had said, "For God so loved the world that He gave His only begotten Son, that whoever believes in Him should not perish but have everlasting life."

Jesus had been saying that just as the Jews in the desert had been bitten by the serpents and were healed by simply looking at the bronze serpent Moses held, so Jesus was being lifted up to bring salvation to anyone who would look to Him. It was as clear as day now. Not only was Jesus the Messiah, but He was also going to be crucified for the sins of the world.

Suddenly he remembered the words of the prophet Isaiah. Seven hundred years earlier, the greatest prophet of all had written about this very moment:

> Surely He has borne our griefs and carried our sorrows; yet we esteemed Him stricken of God and afflicted. But He was wounded for our transgressions, He was bruised for our iniquities; the chastisement for our peace was upon Him, and by His stripes we are healed. All we like sheep have gone astray; we have turned every one, to his own way; And the Lord has laid on Him the iniquity of us all.

Of course it made perfect sense now. Why didn't he see it before? This was not an execution; it was a sacrifice!

Nicodemus now knew what he must do. His job was not to save Jesus. His job was to provide a place of dignity and respect for Jesus after this was all over. And he knew just the man to ask for help.

Finally, Simon dropped the heavy cross where the soldier had ordered. As he turned around, he could see that a huge crowd had joined them. There were men, women, priests, soldiers, and many others who wanted to know what was happening here.

On the way to this place called Golgotha, meaning "the place of the skull," Simon learned a lot. A number of women had gathered together, following them and criying bitterly for this man called Jesus. One of them, named Mary, was Jesus' mother. She was being supported and comforted by several friends, some of whom were also named Mary. *Obviously a popular name around here*, he thought.

Along with the women, there were also several men who followed. These were His disciples. One was named John, and he now stood beside Mary, Jesus' mother. As Simon looked at them, he could see the despair and defeat in their faces. Everything they had ever hoped for was dying here today. Some of the men were actually crying as well.

But the priests weren't crying. They were delighted at what was taking place and actually seemed proud that they had arranged the whole event. Even now, in their cruelty, they continued to hurl insults at the man they were murdering.

Unlike the others, the soldiers didn't seem very interested at all in what was going on. They had seen it all before, and this was just another day at work. At least they would get to keep the clothes the dying men would leave behind.

By now, Simon had learned that Jesus was a prophet who had done good things in Israel. He had taught thousands of people about God and the Kingdom of Heaven. He had healed the sick, fed the hungry, and even raised the dead! As far as Simon knew, He had never done anything wrong! Jesus was here because He had said He was the Messiah. That had been enough for the Pharisees. Even though He had proved what He said with His actions, the Pharisees still didn't believe Him.

As Simon watched, Jesus and two criminals were nailed to crosses and lifted into the air. The screams of pain tore at his ears. The men's agony was unbearable, yet the crucifixion would last for hours.

How could that Pharisee named Levi laugh at all of this? How could anyone laugh at a time like this? Simon wanted to run away, but he couldn't. So he stood there with the others and watched.

"Father, forgive them, for they don't know what they're doing," Jesus said from the cross.

Simon was shocked. How could He pray like this for these monsters? It was almost as if He cared about them.

Above Jesus' head, Pilate had written a sign in three languages that said, "Jesus of Nazareth, The King of the Jews." Simon quietly looked at it. From what he was seeing, he thought, maybe it was true.

As the soldiers gambled for the dying men's clothes, the two criminals on the crosses next to Jesus hurled insults at Him as well. Then a strange thing suddenly happened. As one criminal called across to Jesus, saying, "If you're the Christ, save yourself and us," the other changed his attitude completely. "Don't you fear God, seeing you are under the same condemnation? We deserve what we're getting, but this man has done nothing wrong," he said to the first criminal. Then, turning to Jesus he simply asked, "Lord, remember me when you come into your kingdom."

Simon, who had been watching this go on, could hardly believe his ears as Jesus replied to the man, "I promise you, today you will be with me in Paradise."

As Simon continued to pay attention, he now watched as Jesus turned His attention to His mother and the disciple named John. Mary would need someone to take care of her after Jesus' death. "Woman, behold your son," He said to her. Then He turned to John and said, "Behold your mother." John would now look after Mary for the rest of her life.

One Pharisee in particular did not look like he fit in with the others, Simon noticed. He and another man were off by themselves talking. Though he couldn't hear what they were saying, Simon continued to watch them until the Pharisee turned and saw him. Embarrassed, Simon looked the other way, but the Pharisee called him over.

"I'm sorry, I wasn't trying to listen to your private conversation," Simon apologized.

"That's OK. You're the one who carried His cross, aren't you?" the Pharisee asked.

"Yes, I am," Simon replied. "I'm returning back to my home in Cyrene, but I'd really like to learn more about this Man." he added.

"Then you'll need a place to stay," the Pharisee replied. "My name is Nicodemus, and this is Joseph of Arimathea. Please honor my wife and me by spending the night with us in our home."

As Simon nodded with gratitude, he tried to understand what was happening. Nicodemus continued, "You are wondering who this man on the cross is. We have been watching you, and we can see. Tell us, can you keep a secret?" Simon nodded. He liked these men. They seemed to be good people.

"We are also His disciples," Nicodemus said quietly. "Both Joseph and I believe that even though things look bad, Jesus of Nazareth, the man on the cross, is the Messiah. For the moment, we need to keep this a secret from the Pharisees, but you can trust us. There are many things we need to tell you. We need to leave now to make preparations for His burial. If you wish, you may help us; but I warn you, it could be dangerous." With Simon's nod of agreement, together the three men slipped quietly away. As they did, Nicodemus began to tell Simon things about Jesus that would change his life forever.

Three hours had now passed since Jesus had been lifted up on the cross. It was noon, and still the priests and Pharisees taunted Him and challenged Him to come down from the cross on His own or to call on someone who could help him.

Suddenly, like a blanket of night, darkness descended on the land. Immediately, the taunting stopped. Women gasped in shock. Men waited in fear as everyone wondered what was about to happen. All of Jerusalem lay still in blackness and silence. The only sound came from the groans of pain coming from the three men hanging on crosses in the darkness.

Three more hours passed. Out of the darkness, a wail of suffering and pain was heard as Jesus cried out, "My God, My God, why have You forsaken Me?" To many, it sounded as if Jesus was calling for Elijah the prophet, but they were wrong.

"I'm thirsty," He moaned. Someone raised sour wine up to Him on a hyssop branch. He drank some but it was terrible and did not help.

Finally, in a loud voice, Jesus said His last words from the cross. "It is finished! Father, into Your hands I commit My spirit." Then, bowing His head, He died.

From the darkness, one Roman soldier shook his head as he watched Jesus die. Never had he seen a man die with such courage, grace, and honor. He knew this man Jesus was innocent. "Certainly this was a righteous man," he observed.

Suddenly, at the Temple, the thick, heavy curtain that had separated the Holy of Holies from the Holy Place suddenly split in two from top to bottom. For the first time, everyone in the Temple could see all the way into an area called the Holy of Holies that only the High Priest was permitted to enter once a year. It was as if the secret place was not secret anymore. Immediately, an earthquake began to shake the entire Jerusalem area. Houses crumbled, gates and monuments fell, graveyards opened up, and roads cracked.

Though the centurion at the cross could not see everything that was going on, he could still see enough. In fear and awe he suddenly cried out, "Surely this was the Son of God."

The Jewish leaders, not knowing for certain whether Jesus had died yet, wanted to make sure. So with this in mind, they asked Pilate to ensure that this whole crucifixion process would be finished before the arrival of the Sabbath they were so fond of protecting.

Agreeing, Pilate sent a soldier to check on how things were going at the crosses. After making sure the two thieves died quickly, he approached Jesus and saw that He was indeed dead. Just to make sure, he thrust his spear deep into Jesus' side anyway. He had no idea that he had just fulfilled a prophecy made five hundred years earlier, when the prophet Zechariah said, "They shall look on Him whom they have pierced."

Quietly and without attention, Joseph of Arimathea approached Pilate asking him if he might have the body of Jesus of Nazareth for burial. Meanwhile, Nicodemus and Simon had been arranging the things they would need to bury Jesus' body in a proper and respectful way. With that done, they then headed back to the cross to meet Joseph.

As Pilate listened, the last thing he wanted was to have more trouble with the Jews. So when Joseph requested the body, Pilate agreed to grant his request rather than handing Him over to the hated High Priest and his mob.

Now, with Pilate's permission, Joseph followed the soldiers to the cross. Joseph and Nicodemus waited as the soldiers removed Jesus from the cross, lowering Him to the ground and finally handing His body over to His friends. Carefully, they carried His body the short distance to Joseph's personal tomb that he had already prepared for himself and his family. As Mary Magdalene and the other women waited outside, the men respectfully washed Jesus' body and wrapped Him in clean strips of linen. Finally, with all the preparations completed, they laid Him in Joseph's tomb and rolled a huge stone in front of the door.

The next day was the Sabbath. Surprisingly, the Pharisees chose this day to meet with Pilate, though they usually chose to do as little as possible on the Sabbath. This time, they had one more request. "Sir," they began, "we remember that when this deceiver Jesus was alive, He said that He would rise again in three days. We know, of course, that this would be impossible; however, just in case His disciples might steal the body and say He has risen, we would like you to seal the tomb and to have someone guard it."

"Go ahead," Pilate agreed. "You can use your own guards. Make the tomb as secure as you want."

And so it was done. Jesus was dead. The tomb was sealed. A guard was stationed at the door of the tomb. Pilate was exhausted. The disciples were defeated. The women were in tears, and the Pharisees were positively giddy with joy.

Behind the veil where humans cannot see, every demon lined up to congratulate Satan on his victory. After all this time, he had finally done it. He had won.

And now it was God's turn.

35

Saturday

They all felt the ground shake. Their conversations stopped. Even Abraham, who had been in Paradise the longest, had never felt anything like it. Eli looked over to Moses who simply shrugged his shoulders to indicate that he had no idea what was happening.

Since arriving in Paradise, Rabbi Eli had become close friends with Abraham and Moses. They would often sit together and tell stories about the past. The thing that amazed Eli the most was that even though he had read about these great men for years, there was still so much he didn't know about them. He really enjoyed chatting with them.

Occasionally Rachael dropped by and joined their conversation. The great thing about this was that as they remembered the things that had happened to them on earth, Rachael could help them see how the angels in Heaven had been involved.

Rachael had been the first angel Eli had seen after his death and had given him his first tour of Paradise. Since then, he had gotten to know her better and had gained a whole new appreciation for everything she was doing.

Although she had been created before Adam and Eve and had been involved in many events on earth, she seemed to have grown much wiser and stronger since that day in the Great Palace when Jesus had announced He was going to earth. Abraham, in particular, had noticed the change. It was good to see that even angels continued to grow up.

Even though she was still small when compared to many of the other angels, that didn't matter to her anymore, as it seemed she was becoming more and more confident. Frequently, she had to leave on trips to earth; but when she returned, she would occasionally tell Eli some of the things that were happening to his wife Leah, their children, and of course, Jesus.

There it was again. The tremor; this time it was getting stronger. They all wondered what was happening. And suddenly with a crash, it happened.

Every eye in Paradise watched as the sky above them split in two. The flash was as bright as the sun, and a sound like the call of a trumpet and a crash of thunder shook the entire land. Every conversation stopped in silence as heads looked up to see what was about to happen. Then, every believer who had ever lived and died and come to this place gasped, eyes wide in amazement.

Bursting through the intense light, a man appeared, dressed in shining white robes. His skin was like polished bronze. His bright eyes shone and flashed with intensity and wisdom and purpose.

Unlike them, He had no need of angels to show Him the way to this place. Unlike them, He wasn't the least bit surprised that He had arrived here. He knew where He was and He was at home here.

Though only a few of them, like Eli and John the Baptist, had seen Him on earth, no humans had ever seen Him in Heaven. But there was absolutely no doubt who He was: Jesus, the Messiah, now stood in the sky before them.

As He lifted His hands in the air before them, everyone clearly saw that they had been pierced by nails. As he looked toward them, all could see that His feet also had the same scars.

What had happened? they wondered. *How could this be?*

They would soon find out.

With a voice that rang like thunder, He began to speak. "It is finished," He began. "My sacrifice has been offered, and it has been accepted by My Father."

Jesus turned to Moses and explained, "The Passover Lamb, which was sacrificed that first night in Egypt and then every year thereafter, could never open Heaven for you. It could only cover your sins. Yet year after year, you offered lambs to God in faith. You believed that one day a Deliverer would come who would finally take away your sins forever. That day has now come."

Looking at John the Baptist, He said, "As John, who came before Me taught, I am the Lamb of God that takes away the sins of the world. I was dead but am now alive forevermore, and because I live, you will live with Me."

As Jesus paused, all the saints of Paradise began to shout and cheer with an excitement they had never known. Shouts of "Hallelujah to the Lamb," rang through the rolling hills, and "Praise to Him that lives forevermore," echoed through the streets. Tears of joy poured down faces that were now lifted up in praise to Him, and hands were raised to the sky in victory and honor.

"We have won! We have victory at last!" people shouted again and again as they looked up, hardly able to believe the time had finally come. Jesus had come for them. He had paid the price of their sins and Heaven now waited for their arrival.

Suddenly, another man appeared beside Jesus, who reached out His hand to him. As the man looked around, he seemed dazed and confused, not knowing how he had gotten to this place. *Where am I?* he wondered. Never had he expected this.

"This is My friend," Jesus told them. "He died on a cross beside Me. He believed in Me by calling Me Lord. He repented of his sins in My presence. He asked Me to remember him when I came into My Kingdom. So I have forgiven his sins. I promised him I would bring him here. Because he is forgiven, he will now join us all here as family.

Back in Israel, many people had no idea what had just happened. The disciples, the women, Mary His mother, and many others were still crushed with grief because they had seen Jesus die and felt all their plans had failed. These were the people who needed to have hope again. These were the people who needed to see that victory had truly come. They had no idea that tomorrow they would make a discovery that would change the world forever.

36

Sunday

As the sun rose over the hills of Judea and the morning light began to pour into Jerusalem, the women were already on the move. They had all felt the earthquake during the night that had awakened them, but seeing that there was no damage to their homes, they decided to still carry out their plans. It was dark when they left, but now the light from the sunrise made their path easier to see. They would not be as likely to fall or to twist an ankle on a rock or hole in the ground.

Mary Magdalene arrived first. With her were other women who had helped her make ready the spices they would need to properly prepare Jesus' body for burial.

They still could not believe their best friend was dead. *Why couldn't He save Himself?* they wondered. They had given up everything for Him. What would happen to them now?

Mary saw it first. Something was not right. The stone. It had been moved out of the doorway of the tomb. This was not good. Running to the doorway of the tomb, Mary looked in. Jesus' body was gone. She could not believe it! Just when she thought things couldn't get worse, someone had stolen the body of her Lord. Leaving the other women at the tomb she immediately dashed off to the only other people who might be able to help: Peter and John.

Hearing the knocking on the door, Peter looked out the window carefully. Both he and John had been hiding in fear inside the house since that terrible day when every hope and dream had been snatched away from them. As they hid from the authorities, they were convinced someone would come soon to arrest and crucify them! Peter was still filled with guilt because he had said he didn't know Jesus, and John, thinking he was going to have to move to a safer place, was making preparations to have Mary, Jesus' mother, come and move in with him.

"It's Mary," Peter said as he opened the door to let her in.

As soon as the door was opened, Mary burst into the room, crying, angry, and frustrated. "They've taken Jesus from the tomb and we don't know where He is now!" she gushed.

Peter couldn't believe his ears. "What?" he exclaimed. "Who did this?"

"I don't know," Mary answered, "but He's gone!"

Peter, as impulsive as ever, exploded out the door, yelling for John to follow him. Running as fast as they could to the tomb, they forgot about Mary who was trying to keep up with them.

Arriving at the tomb first, John rushed to the open door and looked inside. On his right side, where Jesus had been, lay the strips of cloth, or grave clothes, that had been used to wrap Jesus' body. But Jesus was gone. Arriving behind him, Peter squeezed passed John and went right into the tomb to see for himself. No Jesus.

Now John began noticing things that the others had missed! The grave clothes and even the head covering were still there and not on Jesus' body. It was as if Jesus' body had vanished into thin air and His grave clothes had just collapsed where the body had been. This was strange. If someone had taken Jesus' body, surely they would not have taken the time to remove all the cloth wrappings. And even if they had, the cloth would be strewn all over the floor, not the way they lay now. But that was clearly not what had happened here. Suddenly John knew; this was no grave robbery. He had no idea how, but Jesus was somehow alive.

Unknown to Mary, Peter, and John, the soldiers who had been guarding Jesus' tomb, who were still terrified by what they had seen, were at this very moment telling the chief priests their unbelievable story. "We were standing guard in front of the tomb when the earthquake hit! That wasn't a problem. We have all seen earthquakes before. However, then Marcus saw him. Then I saw him too. An angel, descending out of the sky, appeared right in front of us! He was huge. Maybe eight or nine feet tall, dressed in pure white and shining like lightening.

"He rolled the stone in front of tomb's door away, as if it was no heavier than a leaf. Then he just sat down on the stone and faced us. We were so afraid we fell on the ground. Then everything went black. We must have passed out. When we regained consciousness, we checked the tomb, but it was empty. After this, we came to you immediately."

This was not good news for the priests. Just when they thought they had gotten rid of this Rabbi from Nazareth, his body disappeared. They had to come up with an explanation quickly. Hastily putting together as much money as they could find, they gave it to the guards. "Look, if anyone asks about this, tell them, 'His disciples came at night and stole His body while we slept.' We'll make sure you don't get in trouble with the governor." And so it was that the lie claiming that Jesus' disciples had stolen His body started circulating.

But it would not be so easy to explain what happened next. Peter and John had left the tomb. They would need to talk this over among themselves and get together with the others.

Mary found herself alone again at the tomb. She had come here to do one last kind thing for her Lord Jesus, and now she couldn't even do that. She was convinced that someone had taken Him away, and with that thought in her mind, she again broke down in tears. Now she needed to leave for home, but before she left, she would look one more time in the tomb.

The sight of the two angels almost dropped her to her knees in fear.

"Why are you weeping?" Rachael asked her.

"Because they've taken away my Lord, and I don't know where He is," Mary replied.

The sight of the angels suddenly appearing inside the tomb had shocked her, and she pulled back outside as if to check from where they had come.

Turning her head, Mary saw a man near the tomb. The gardener, she thought. Maybe he might know something. Before she could ask, He asked the same question that Rachael had. "Why are you weeping? Who are you looking for?"

Mary, exhausted now, simply blurted out her request. "Sir, if you have carried Him away, tell me where You have laid Him, and I will go get Him."

It only took her name. "Mary," He said, and she knew. It was Jesus.

"Rabboni!" she shouted. The word meant "Teacher," and it was what she had so often called him when He was alive. Unable to even think about what she was doing, she leapt at Him, wrapping her arms around Him.

"Hey there, don't cling to me now Mary," Jesus said, smiling. "I need to go to My Father now. You go and tell My disciples I'm ascending to My Father who is My God and your God."

Pulling herself away from Him, Mary could hardly believe her eyes. He was alive! He was really alive! He had not left her alone after all. He was back. And now she had people to tell.

Rachael and Gabriel smiled as they watched her go. They knew she had gone through a difficult time when Jesus had died. Now they saw the excitement on her face as she realized that Jesus was indeed alive. It was an amazing thing for them to see.

The angels left the tomb knowing they would see Mary Magdalene later. Then, she and others who would see Jesus alive again would share their amazing stories. Jesus was alive, and they had seen Him and touched Him. They would rush to tell anyone who would listen and their stories would change people's lives forever.

Jesus had already appeared to Mary Magdalene at the tomb and soon He would appear to the other disciples as well. But now He was going to His Father, and He was going to bring with Him those who had trusted Him.

Back in Paradise, Jesus stood again before the thousands and thousands of saints who had died through the ages, waiting for the

Messiah to finally make a way for their sin to be forgiven. Now that way had been opened. Jesus had paid for their sins by dying on the cross, and now He had risen from the dead.

As shouts of praise from the saints of Paradise continued to ring through the land, a huge staircase leading up to Heaven appeared before them.

"Come," Jesus called. "Come with Me now and meet My Father. See, Heaven is now open!" He exclaimed. As He spoke these words, the sky opened around Him to reveal a throne and the One who sat on the throne. Thousands upon thousands of angels stood around it praising God, saying, "Blessed is the Lamb who was slain, and worthy is He to receive honor and praise and glory."

Now the saints of Paradise saw a great Holy Temple made of gold that surrounded the throne. Its gates were made of pearl and its streets, which led in and out of the gates, were paved with gold. There was a gigantic sea of glass before the Great Temple that shimmered in the light. There were precious jewels everywhere, and the people heard music that was more beautiful than anything on earth or even in Paradise.

Rachael watched as thousands of people who had been living in Paradise raced up the stairs to Heaven and into the Great Palace. Jesus had done it. He had come to earth and rescued those who could not rescue themselves. From the time the first man and woman decided to disobey God, sin had kept people from being able to be truly at peace with God. The penalty of sin was always death, but because every person had sinned, no one could ever save themselves. But that had all changed now. Jesus had died for each person, paying that price Himself, and now the power of sin was broken. Heaven was open to every person who was willing to receive the gift of life Jesus was offering.

As he raced up the stairs, Eli saw Rachael and grinned at her. She had told him that something better was coming, and now it was here. Continuing the climb, he looked ahead to the top of the stairs. Jesus was there, and Eli wanted to meet Him again.

As he reached the top, Jesus looked at him and smiled. "Eli, my friend, I told you we would meet again soon, didn't I?" Eli shook his head in amazement. Never could he have imagined it would be like this. Wrapping his arms around Jesus and weeping for joy he hugged the One he had taught as a child and had watched grow into a man. As he climbed the rest of the way with Jesus, the Paradise saints finally entered Heaven together.

Now a new smell reached them. Incense. They had smelled incense on earth before, of course, but never anything like this. It was fresh and clean and exhilarating and reminded them of mint and cinnamon and cloves. This was a heavenly incense, for it represented the very presence of God. It was so incredibly refreshing, it made each breath exciting and each person there just wanted to keep breathing it in. This was what God smelled like.

Something else was new in Heaven that they had not known in Paradise: the presence of Jesus.

Because God can be everywhere at the same time, even though there were millions of angels and saints there, no one had to wait in line to talk to Him. He was never too busy when someone wanted Him. He was just there. Although it took some getting used to, it was very cool.

Something else the Paradise saints had to get used to was that nothing ever got old. Even the excitement they had felt when they first arrived at this amazing place had not gone away.

Eli had been thinking for some time how wonderful it would be to see his wife again. As a matter of fact, he couldn't wait. He could only imagine the look on her face when she saw all of this. But that would come soon enough. Now there were things to do, and he needed to see Abraham.

Rachael and Gabriel now stood in the Great Palace before Jesus. As one of the two most powerful and important angels in Heaven, this was not new for Gabriel. Rachael, however, was excited beyond words. With her were Naomi and Gideon, her true friends who had helped her often.

"I want to thank you for all you have done for Me," Jesus began. "When you learned that I would become a man, you were disappointed and didn't want Me to go," He said, looking at Rachael. "But now you have seen how important it was that I went and did what had to be done, just as the prophets wrote of in the Scriptures. Even though you didn't understand everything that was happening, you trusted Me and were there to help and serve. Because of this, millions of people are now in Heaven with us. Look, Rachael, at what you have helped Me do."

Looking up, Rachael could see the thousands and thousands of people who were now gathered together in Heaven. Men, women, and children filled this vast new space, smiling, full of joy, and still amazed that they were here! There was no sickness or poverty or pain. There were no sounds of crying, not even from the small children there. There was no fear, and for the first time, they had found real peace. They were now living in the very presence of God. Jesus had done all of this, and she had helped.

As Rachael looked down shyly, Jesus continued to speak. "This is not the end of the story yet Rachael," He said, smiling at her. "In many ways this is just the beginning. Before I return to earth again, at the time of the end, many hundreds of years will pass. Many will learn about Me and what I have done for them. Those who have followed Me on earth will tell others about what I have done and how they may know they have eternal life. These new believers will then tell others and they, in turn, will tell others. All over the world, men, women, and even children will learn of My Father and of Me. Even though the world will hate them for it, many will receive Me as their Savior. Around the world they will become known as Christians, but to Me, as they meet together to remember Me and to love one another, these people will be called My Church."

Then, placing His arm around her shoulders, just above her wings, Jesus said, "You've done well, Rachael. Would you like to continue to help? I have a Church that needs to be built."

Jesus thanks Rachael for all she has done.

Bible Passages for Further Study

Part 1: The Journey from the Great Palace

CHAPTER 1

Exodus 12:3-7
Leviticus 12:8; 16:22
Isaiah 53:5, 11
Daniel 7:10; 9:21; 10:13
Matthew 1:23
Luke 1:26-38; 2:8-16
John 3:16
Acts 5:3-4
Galatians 1:3
Hebrews 1:8
Revelation 21:21

CHAPTER 2

Isaiah 7:14
Micah 5:2
Matthew 1:18-25; 18:10
Luke 2:7-16

CHAPTER 3
Micah 5:2
Matthew 2
Luke 2:39

CHAPTER 4
Jonah 1:3

CHAPTER 5
Job 38:4, 7
Isaiah 14:12-15
Luke 10:18
Revelation 12:4

CHAPTER 6
Genesis 1:27-30; 2:8-9, 16-17; 3:1-19, 23-24
Ezekiel 28:17

CHAPTER 7
Exodus 1:13-14; 2:1-10; 3:7, 10; 4:29-31; 5:1-4; 7:20-21; 8:6,15-19, 24, 32; 9:6, 8-35; 10:3-29; 12:6, 12-13, 15, 21-24, 31-32

CHAPTER 8
John 1:29
Hebrews 1:8

CHAPTER 9
Hosea 11:1
Matthew 2:20-23

Luke 1:39-40
Jude 16:4

CHAPTER 10

Psalm 14:3
Isaiah 59:12
Jeremiah 17:9
Luke 15:7, 10; 2:25-35, 42-49
2 Timothy 3:16
1 Peter 2:22

Part 2: The Journey from the Great Palace Continues

CHAPTER 11

Mark 6:3
Luke 3:23
John 8:56

CHAPTER 12

Matthew 3:1, 2, 7, 13-17
Mark 1:6, 12-13
John 1:20-28

CHAPTER 13

Genesis 7:12
Joshua 5:6
1 Kings 19:8
Matthew 4:1-12

CHAPTER 14

John 1:35-45; 2:1-12

CHAPTER 15

Matthew 2:16

CHAPTER 16

Luke 4:16-21, 28-41

John 2:13-21, 23

CHAPTER 17

John 3:2-10, 14-16

CHAPTER 18

Numbers 21:5-9

CHAPTER 19

John 3:22; 4:3-4

CHAPTER 20

Luke 16:19-31

Part 3: The Journey Home to the Great Palace Begins

CHAPTER 21

John 4:4-42, 46-53

CHAPTER 22
Mark 1:14; 2:13-17; 3:1-6
Luke 5:17-25

CHAPTER 23
John 5:1-15

CHAPTER 24
Matthew 5:1-12, 27-28; 6:5-13; 7:21-23; 8:1-3, 5-13
Mark 1:23-27, 29-31, 40-45
John 2:1-10; 4:46-53; 5:1-15
Romans 3:23
1 Peter 2:22

CHAPTER 25
Isaiah 35:4-6
Psalm 103:3; 146:8
Hosea 13:14
Matthew 8:23-27
Mark 4:35-41
Luke 7:11-23, 36-50

CHAPTER 26
Deuteronomy 18:15, 18
Matthew 14:22, 28-32
Mark 6:14-29
John 6:2-21

CHAPTER 27
John 16:26-28, 35; 7:24, 37, 38, 45-52
Hebrews 13:5

CHAPTER 28
John 8:1-11

CHAPTER 29
John 9:2-38

CHAPTER 30
John 10:14-18; 11:1-44

CHAPTER 31
Zechariah 9:9
Matthew 26:6, 26-30
Luke 22:1-16
John 11:45-53; 12:1-19; 13:1-11, 21-30, 34-35; 14:1-3, 6; 15:1-2; 16:1-4; 17

CHAPTER 32
Matthew 26:31-49, 52-53
Luke 22:43, 51
John 18:1, 3-13

CHAPTER 33
Matthew 26:57-67, 74-75; 27:1-2, 19, 24
Luke 22:63-71; 23:6-15
John 18:17, 19-23, 28-39; 19:1-6, 12-16

CHAPTER 34

Isaiah 53:5-6
Zechariah 12:10
Matthew 27:33, 35, 41-46, 61-66
Mark 15:21, 32
Luke 23:27, 39-43, 46-47, 51-54
John 19:25-27, 30, 38-42

CHAPTER 35

Luke 23:39-43
Ephesians 4:8-9
1 Peter 4:5-6

CHAPTER 36

Matthew 28:2, 11-15
Luke 23:1; 24:1-10
John 20:1-18
Acts 7:56

ABOUT THE AUTHOR

Bob Wilkinson was born in St. John's, Newfoundland and spent his early years growing up in a small fishing outport there. Later he moved to Regina, Saskatchewan where he started high school. He also took flight classes that would one day lead him to a career as an airline pilot. He became a captain at the age of twenty-five and piloted for over forty years.

While serving as a captain, he devoted his time to aviation safety. He was on several safety committees. He was also an accident investigator with special emphasis on human factors investigation and personal counseling.

A few years later, Bob became a believer in Jesus Christ. He enrolled at Liberty University's Home Bible Institute and graduated from there with a two-year Bible diploma. He has developed a keen interest in Christian apologetics, creation, and Biblical history, and now uses this training in his role as a Bible teacher. While in Israel, he has conducted many tours of the country, giving participants a new and up-close appreciation of the land of the Bible.

Today, Bob is retired from the airline but continues to teach students at a flight college. He is still active in his local church. He lives with his wife, Shelagh, at their home in Tidnish, Nova Scotia.

Journey from the Great Palace is his first book.

Readers can connect with Bob Wilkinson at:
rwilkinson767@gmail.com

CPSIA information can be obtained at www.ICGtesting.com
Printed in the USA
BVOW01s2200130916

462020BV00002B/6/P

9 781940 269771